RESCUED BY LOVE

Park City Firefighter Romance

CAMI CHECKETTS

Birch River Publishing

Birch River Publishing

Smithfield, Utah

Published in the United States of America

Cover design: Steven Novak

Interior design: Memphis Checketts

Editing: Daniel Coleman

To my Daddy for always telling me that nobody wants to dance with a girl with skinny legs.

INTRODUCTION

A Conversation from Summer 2016

3 Bestselling Authors (Checketts, Hart, and Kersey): Hey Daniel, we're writing a firefighter romance series. Do you want in?

Me (on the inside): Yes I totally do, oh, I can't wait, how long should my book be, when should I have it done holy cow you ladies are the greatest ever of all time!

Me (on the outside): Cool. Why me?

3 Bestselling Authors: You're a firefighter. Oh, and uh, you have mad writing and editing skills.

3 Bestselling Authors (to each other): Should we tell him Nicolas Sparks wasn't available?

Six months, seven million emails, and dozens of interviews later, four Park City Firefighter Romance books are ready to thrill you, touch you, inspire you, and make you swoon.

In my 15 years on the job, I've worked side-by-side with over a thousand of America's Bravest. The men and women I've known make excellent studies for romance characters because they are fit, selfless, daring, passionate and without exception—imperfect. Kersey, Hart, and Checketts (dare I include myself?) have captured the essence of the beautifully flawed lives that so often result from a career that injects its members into the public's worst day. When true love is added to the mix, sparks fly and things really heat up.

Experience the bravery, the struggle, the emotional pain, and the passion of heroes as they face their fears, their demons, and their pasts en route to finding lasting love. It may just surprise you who is the hero and who is the one in need of rescue.

It is my pleasure to introduce the Park City Firefighter Romance Series.

CHAPTER ONE

Though he kept a solemn look on his face, Captain Cameron Christian Compton, or Quad C as pretty much everyone on C Platoon called him, was laughing inside. They'd just been dispatched to a wreck on I-80, close to the Tanger Outlet stores on the west side of Park City, and his engineer, Emily, had squeaky toys in her boots, again. She squeaked as she rushed to the truck.

It was probably JFK who had pulled the prank. He lived to tease, especially when interacting with attractive women. Cam would need to reprimand him later, but the dose of humor was necessary, or they'd all go insane dealing with the stress and high pressure.

"Again?" he asked Emily.

"Sorry, Cap." She shook her head. "I figured we were in too big of a hurry for me to take off all my gear and start over."

"Not your fault."

They were at the accident in minutes. Several police cars were already there. Old Guy and Link were right behind them in the ambulance and quickly carried a gurney down the hill. It had rained quite a bit earlier today, and the Cherokee must've hydroplaned then hit a dry spot and rolled down the embankment. An older lady stood outside the car shrieking about her granddaughter. Cam reached the wreckage first. The young brunette was struggling to get free, but it looked like her legs were pinned.

"Calm down, ma'am." Cam instructed. "We'll get you out soon."

Her door was smashed, so he rushed around to the passenger side and muscled the door open wider, wondering how the grandmother had slipped out of that narrow opening. Cam shimmied into the car, pulled a knife out, and cut the seat belt.

"Thank you," the girl whispered. Her brown eyes filled with tears. "I can't get my leg free." She pointed to her left leg.

"No worries." He glanced over the smashed dashboard and steering wheel. If he cut away part of the dashboard, they could get her out, but they needed more room to work to avoid manipulating her back in case she'd suffered any spinal injuries.

He hollered to the new boot, Powers. "Grab the Jaws and cut open the driver's side."

"Got it, Cap." He pounded back up the hill.

"We're going to get you out," Cam told the woman.

She grasped his hand and held on tight. "Please don't leave me."

Cam nodded. Powers and JFK were completely capable of cutting the door off and lifting the dashboard away. At least he hoped. Last shift, less than a week ago, they'd gone over the procedure ... on paper. Cam squeezed her hand. "Sure. You're going to be fine."

"Thanks." She licked her lips and looked at him beseechingly. "Are you married?"

Cam pulled back, but she clung to him. What kind of a question was that? He looked past her to his crew, pulling out the Jaws and making their way back to him. "No."

"Oh, good." She blinked up at him. "You're really hot, and I was hoping I could make you some cookies to thank you for rescuing me. My applesauce cookies are almost as yummy as you." She licked her lips. Cam thought she must not be in much pain to be flirting like this, so that was at least one good aspect of this embarrassing situation. On the other hand, maybe it meant she had hit her head really hard.

JFK stood next to the open door where Cam was wedged. Cam glanced up at him for help, though he should've known better.

"She's pretty cute, Cap. I'd take cookies from her."

Cam grunted. JFK was an idiot. Cam didn't want to upset the girl during quite possibly one of the most traumatic moments of her life. "Thanks. I'd love ... cookies."

She smiled and leaned her head back against the headrest and kept staring at him. It was beyond awkward. JFK smirked as he handed a white sheet to Cam then hurried around the car to help Powers. Emily ran the hydraulic generator as Cam's firefighters made strategic cuts to the A and B posts. The wrenching of metal was comforting to Cam. He covered the girl with the sheet to protect her from breaking glass and stayed in his awkward position as the girl clung to his hand. She occasionally smiled or winked at him, though it was obvious she was scared and uncomfortable.

His crew cut the door away like it was made of cardboard then stuck in the spreaders and lifted the dashboard. Even after eight years of doing this, Cam loved the procedure of removing a car from around a patient. It was a beautiful thing to see his crew in action, working as a team to carry out a textbook procedure and getting it done so efficiently.

Link and Old Guy were on hand with a C-collar and a gurney. They slid a long spine board under the patient and, with Cam's help, carefully positioned her on the board. Luckily, she had to release Cam's hand as they pulled her out of the peeled open side of the car. Cam slid out the other side and came around to follow the gurney. The grandma was by her granddaughter's side, still crying as the girl reassured her that she was doing okay.

They lifted the girl into the ambulance. "I'll be by with cookies, hot firefighter guy." She called to Cam.

The police, paramedics, and other firefighters all gave him smirks or outright laughed at him. The grandmother turned to him and threw her arms around him. Cam stood stiffly. He wasn't used to much physical contact. His sister, Caylee, hugged him every chance she got, but she was in California for school, so he didn't see her often.

"Thank you for saving her. We love you."

Cam patted her awkwardly, half-disappointed when she released him. Old Guy assisted the grandma into the ambulance. Powers jumped in behind him to be on hand for the ride down to Salt Lake.

Link slammed the doors and hurried around to the driver's side. The policemen drifted away, but Cam stayed in place, and his crew all stood around him, awaiting his instructions. The hug and profession of love from the elderly lady shook him. Why was he thinking of Grandma when he needed to focus on work?

"Dang, Cap. You always get the women chasing you." JFK shook his head in disgust.

Emily rolled her eyes. "JFK, nobody wants to get hit on in an emergency situation."

"Thanks." Cam nodded to Emily. She shifted her weight, and her boots squeaked. "And nobody wants to sound like a chew toy on an emergency scene." He gave JFK a pointed stare. "The joke's old."

"*What?*" JFK lifted a shoulder and hid a grin. That was high acknowledgment for him. He'd changed the prank to something different next time. Cam was just grateful his mouth wasn't running for a few seconds.

"Let's clean up and get out of here." Cam ordered. Everyone scampered to obey. He still thought it was interesting that a cute girl smiling and offering to make him cookies held little appeal to him, but a grandma hugging him brought a desire for family he hadn't indulged in for years. He shook himself and went to help his crew.

CHAPTER TWO

Sage Turner pulled up to Park City Clothing Company on Main Street, glancing around desperately for a parking spot. Downtown was too stinking busy. Ski season was over, but the mountain biking and hiking had begun. Tourists adored her hometown, and she didn't mind sharing, *most* of the time.

There was a red zone not too far from the store. She shouldn't do it, but it was either park illegally, drive around until something opened up, or drive to the parking lot at the base of Main Street and run to the store. She didn't mind running, but she was in a hurry to get back and help her mom, who was stressed about looking perfect for Luke Free-stone's party. She'd be two seconds in the store, and then she'd be back out.

Jamming her Jeep into gear, she leaned back and breathed in the fresh Park City air. Hallelujah that it was finally warm enough to have the soft top off. Her parents thought she was nuts driving a Wrangler around a mountain valley that was frozen a good portion of the time, but she loved it. It was still cool this time of year, high of seventy if they were lucky, perfect weather to have your top off. She could wear a coat and gloves while she drove. It was worth it to be able to taste the crisp air.

Jumping down, she patted her Jeep fondly. She'd restored it with her brother, and now that he was deployed, the Jeep was the remembrance of him she needed when the days without him got lonely.

She sprinted into the store. Her mom had begged her to run in and get her Wolford tights for her dinner party tonight. Her mom was in a tizzy about being invited to Luke Freestone's mansion. Her parents had been friends with Luke's dad, John, for years, but hadn't had much contact with his sons. Sage had always thought all the Freestone brothers were good guys, but she had to roll her eyes at another request when her mom had twenty pairs of Wolford's in her lingerie drawer. With her dad's fibromyalgia getting worse every day, Sage wanted to help them however she could.

She found the tights within seconds, groaning at the long line snaking toward the cash register. Pasting on a smile, she hoped some random cop didn't drive by and see her parked in the red zone. Most of the cops in town knew her Jeep and had given her a ticket at one time or another.

An older lady with blue-tinged white hair turned around and grinned at her. "You want to go in front of me, sweetheart?"

"Oh, no, I'm fine." Had her worry been that evident? "I just parked in the red zone."

The lady laughed, and her eyes twinkled. "As long as those hunky firemen don't come by, you'll be just fine."

"I'm more worried about a policeman than a fireman." Firemen? Oh, wouldn't that be her luck.

The lady waved her hand. "Beautiful girl like you could talk them out of any ticket. Just flash them one of those long legs."

Sage grinned at her, even though the reference to her long legs wasn't necessarily a compliment. She'd been called everything from giraffe to giant. "I wish. I talk myself blue, but they always give me a ticket." Her brother, Levi, on the other hand, got out of every ticket. He never groveled like she did, simply greeted the policeman with his friendly grin and said, "Do your worst. I probably deserve it." Everybody loved her brother. For some reason, police seemed to have a radar where she was concerned. Maybe it was because she adored her Jeep so

much and reveled in driving fast with the top off. She'd gotten a repu-
tation with the local law enforcement during high school, and it hadn't
gotten much better since she'd graduated from the University of Utah
and moved back to Park City to teach fourth grade at Parley's Park
Grade School. She reminded herself constantly to be a good example
to her students, but sometimes a girl just needed to cruise.

Sirens cut through the air. Sage jumped, and the lady's eyes
widened. "Firefighters," she whispered.

Sage calmed her breathing. They weren't coming for her. Firefighters lived to help people, not cuss a Jeep owner for parking illegally.

The distinctive smell of smoke wafted through the store, and
smoke detectors started going off throughout the shop. Sage glanced
up at the sprinklers and hoped they weren't going to start spraying.

"We'd better get a move on, sweetheart," the lady said.

Sage hooked her arm through the older lady's, having to stoop
considerably as she was five feet and eleven point eight inches, but the
elderly lady probably didn't even clear five feet. She hurried with her
new friend to the exit, now blocked with all the people who'd been in
line or were browsing the store's merchandise.

"The fire is in the restaurant next door." A loud voice boomed.
"Exit in an orderly fashion and please move to the south down the
sidewalk."

Sage peered over other women's heads to see the fire truck parked
parallel to her Jeep and the firefighters pulling their hoses. One really
porky firefighter made rude gestures to her vehicle. She wanted to wilt
right into the floor. Please don't let them realize it was her that had
been too impatient to find a parking spot. She had thought she could
just run in and out quickly. Why had she done that? Dumb,
dumb, dumb.

They cleared the door, and the lady whispered, "Ooh, they're not
happy with that Jeep, are they?"

Sage shook her head, her face blazing hot. Why had she parked
there? She'd been afraid of a parking ticket, but had never even
thought of a fire. The porky guy dragged the hose from the fire truck
and flung it over the top of her jeep. Another firefighter hooked into

the hydrant as Sage and her new friend shuffled south of the store and watched the action. Smoke seeped out of the restaurant next door, but it didn't look like a huge blaze. A couple more firefighters ran into the restaurant. She guessed they were checking to make sure the people were all out.

The hose went taut as it filled with water. Before dragging the hose the rest of the way to the building, Porky drenched her Jeep. Just opened the nozzle right up and sprayed the interior of her vehicle.

"Hey!" Sage screamed. She disconnected from the lady and ran to save her baby.

The hose turned off and Porky whirled around to glare at her. "You're the idiot—Oh, hey, pretty, gargantuan woman." He eyed her up and down and puffed out his chest. "I got a little fire to take care of. Then you and me could exchange some digits."

"You just soaked my Jeep!"

"Oh, sorry. Shouldn't of parked there." The other fireman ran up, and together they dragged the hose off into the building. Porky turned to give her a broad wink before he entered.

Sage stood rooted to the concrete. She knew she shouldn't have parked there, but was soaking her beloved Jeep really warranted?

Firefighters, shouting, and smoke streamed around her as she stared into her Jeep, the floor was flooded with water. Did he ruin her Sony stereo system or Bluetooth? Would the leather seats recover? At least the floors were made of rubber, but the rest wasn't, and it made her sick to think of Porky desecrating it like that.

The fire must've been small, like she'd originally thought, because the firefighters came back out pretty quickly. The first two in uniform were a beautiful girl and model-gorgeous guy. They walked past together, giving her slightly annoyed looks. She was formulating a groveling apology when Porky strode back out.

He handed the hose off to Model Man. "Here, Boot. Load it up." Then he came right into Sage's personal space. She had him by an inch, and she could tell it bugged him. "Heya, my beautiful Amazon. You realize we could've broken your windows or rolled this Jeep over, but I held the guys back because that's the kind of guy I am."

"You mean a loser?" The firefighter girl taunted him. "Shut it, JFK and get in the truck."

"I'm working something here."

"Working a rejection." She shot back. She and Model Man strode away to the truck.

"What do you think, my gargantuan Barbie Doll?" Porky grinned at her. "You buy me dinner to make up for parking in our way?"

"In your daydreams." Sage managed to get out. Who was this loser, and how dare he keep making fun of her height? Didn't men realize she hated being taller than them more than they hated having insecurities about it?

"Ah, come on, don't be like that. I got a lot of buddies on the police force. You wanna parking ticket, or you wanna have dinner with a firefighting stud?"

A true firefighting stud appeared on the threshold of the restaurant, and the sight of him sucked the oxygen out of Sage. He wasn't picture perfect like Model Man. He was the kind of rugged handsome that belonged on a mountain man poster, minus the beard. He'd look good with a beard too, but she really liked seeing his tanned face. He had a look that let a woman know he would rescue her from a mountain lion and make her sigh with longing at the same time. His eyes were almost a navy blue, dark and full of promise. His lips were well formed with a nice arch on the top and a full lower lip. He zeroed in on her, and she stumbled a bit.

Porky reached out a hand to steady her. "Hey now, beautiful. I know I have an effect, but don't go falling into my arms when I'm on the clock. You're big enough I might not be able to catch you."

"Get in the truck, JFK." Mountain Man ordered.

"Ah, Cap, you're ruining my play here."

"Truck, now." He didn't even raise his voice, but the command in that bass made Sage back up a step.

Porky groaned, but stomped around her Jeep. "I'll find you later, Hot Gigantor," He called back to her.

Sage ignored him, completely focused on Mountain Man and wondering what he was going to do to her. She'd parked her Jeep in the way of a fire truck, and this guy was obviously in command. He slowly walked toward her. The turnout coat and pants made him look even bigger than he probably was, but she could tell he was built, and it wasn't fluff like Porky.

As he came closer, she found herself slowly backing away. She hit her Jeep and couldn't go anywhere. He stopped a couple of feet away, not getting into her space like Porky had, but she still felt surrounded by him—the commanding way he carried himself and the dangerous glint in his eyes.

"I-I'm sorry?" She squeaked out.

He arched an eyebrow. "Sorry for JFK hitting on you?"

She shook her head quickly and gestured toward her sopping wet vehicle.

"This is your Jeep." Understanding lit his eyes. "And JFK was going to rip you a new one until he saw how gorgeous you are."

She bit at her lip. He'd just called her gorgeous. He was tall enough he wasn't intimidated by her height, yet he didn't look too friendly. She was obviously in the wrong here, but it ticked her off that Porky, or JFK, had sprayed her vehicle.

"Okay, I know I shouldn't have parked here. I was just running in quickly, and your guy acted like a total dipwad and sprayed the interior of my Jeep. Look!" She gestured behind her.

He took another step closer, and now she really couldn't breathe. Peering over her shoulder, he blew out a breath. "That was uncalled for, but you do realize it's illegal to park in front of a fire hydrant?" He glanced down at her, and her thoughts scattered. The way he was looking at her should be illegal. All smoky hot and stern at the same time. She'd never understood the obsession with powerful authority figures, but this guy just had it going on.

"Is it legal to damage private property?"

His eyebrows lifted again. "No. Did JFK damage your Jeep?"

She wasn't sure yet. Luckily, the floor was rubber, and she should be able to clean it up if she worked hard, but the seats and the stereo could be a different story. "I'll probably have to detail it, and the stereo and leather seats might be ruined."

His eyes swept over her. "Come over to the station with a bill for any damage and the detail, and I'll make sure JFK pays it."

She'd just bet he would make sure. How would anybody ever tell this guy no? She almost felt like he'd issued her a challenge. Come see me again sometime, or something like that. It definitely wasn't over-done or creepy like Porky. It was seductive, and she wouldn't mind seeing him again sometime at all. Yet there was no way she'd go to the station and face all those firefighters again. They probably all hated her for parking in their way.

"I just might," she said, putting as much sass as she could manage into her tone.

He grinned, and she clung to the side mirror for support. His smile made him so appetizing she wanted to beg his forgiveness for being in their way and beg him to let her take him to dinner as penance like Porky had suggested she do with him.

"I'll look forward to it, ma'am." He touched the brim of his fire-fighter hat thing, and she could've sworn she'd been transported to an old John Wayne film. She had to remind herself that she was a capable, twenty-first century woman, not the little sweetie who fawned over the big old Mountain Man/Cowboy/Hot Firefighter.

He gave her one more grin before striding around her Jeep and climbing into the passenger side of their huge fire rig. Sage stood still and watched him go.

"See you later, beautiful." Porky called out from the back seat.

Sage focused on her Mountain Man and loved that he glanced her way and gave her one more devastating smile before they roared away.

"Well, sweetheart." The older lady from the store was suddenly standing right next to her. "It could've been a lot worse than a fine-looking firefighter giving you the what for."

"Yes, it could have."

"I'd take a reaming from that man any day o' the week." She fanned herself.

Sage giggled, relieved it had gone so well and replaying every look that man had given her and every word he'd uttered. "I didn't mind it at all."

"You'd better go and see him at the fire station. Take him a treat, and I bet that grin he gives you then will be even more sexy." She lowered her voice conspiratorially.

Sage wasn't sure that grin could get any sexier. She thought of her mom's "Knock You Naked Brownies," stolen from the Pioneer Woman's website, and smiled. She would turn on the sugar and see if that commanding man could be softened up, and maybe, if she was really lucky, he'd ask her out.

CHAPTER THREE

Monday morning, Cam parked his quad-cab truck in the visitor parking space of the grade school and slowly climbed out. Children were some of his favorite people in the world, but he didn't like talking in front of adults. Maybe he could ask the teacher to let him talk to her class alone. He sighed. Yeah, like that was going to happen. Leave twenty-five nine and ten-year-olds alone with someone she didn't know. At least the material was as familiar as JFK's nonstop chatter.

He checked in with the front desk, put his guest tag on, and sauntered down the hallway. Arriving at his assigned classroom, he wondered what Miss Turner would be like. She'd emailed him a few weeks ago requesting he come talk to her class about fire safety. They'd started an email conversation that he had enjoyed more than he wanted to admit. He didn't really converse with people outside his fire crew, his sister, the boys on his lacrosse team, and the mom who organized the youth lacrosse teams. He'd gotten to know her when she had a small electrical fire at her house, and she'd recruited him to coach six years ago.

In writing, Miss Turner was witty and well-spoken. As he'd gotten to know her a little bit through the emails, she'd made him laugh with her quips about overbearing firefighters and policemen who liked to give her tickets because she had a lead foot. He wondered how she would've reacted if she would've been the beauty with the red Jeep on Saturday. He smiled thinking about how well that lady had dealt with JFK's blatant flirtations and hadn't even blinked an eye when Cam called her gorgeous. She'd probably heard that so much she didn't even notice anymore. She was the type of woman men wrote poetry about —the smooth skin, the full lips, and the long, blonde hair. He loved the contrast of her deep brown eyes. He'd fantasized about her all weekend and called himself all kinds of shallow. He'd been completely intrigued by the sassy schoolteacher Miss Turner. Then he saw an unreal beauty, and all of a sudden, she was all he could think about.

He scowled at himself as he pounded on the door. He wasn't looking for a relationship anyway, so what did it matter? His sister claimed he needed to put their past behind him and find a woman, but it was much smarter and safer just to work at the fire station and coach his youth lacrosse team. He wondered if any of his players would be in Miss Turner's class as she swung the door wide.

"Come in ..." Her voice trailed off, and she blinked up at him.

Cam was at a loss for words too. Miss Turner was his beauty who drove a Jeep and parked in front of fire hydrants. She was tall, probably close to six feet, but he had her by at least four inches. He found himself puffing his chest out similar to what JFK would've done, but luckily his sister Caylee's voice was in his head, *Come on, dude, don't act like a hormonal teenager.*

"Mountain Man," she whispered.

Cam gave a surprised chuckle. Her comment broke any worry he'd had about how to respond. "Excuse me?"

"I mean, Captain Compton. Welcome." She backed away from the door and gestured him inside.

"Thank you, Miss Turner." He couldn't stop his voice from going all deep, and he couldn't swing his eyes away from her.

She was blushing a lovely pink as she deliberately turned from him. "Class, this is Captain Compton—"

"Coach!" The yell came from the back of the classroom, but Cam knew exactly who it was. He heard that yell thirty times a practice.

"Braden." He greeted his player with a smile.

Braden waved enthusiastically from across the room. "He's my lacrosse coach," he proudly told the boy next to him.

The boy nodded respectfully. "Lucky."

Cam's smile grew. Braden was one of his favorite players. The boy had a hard time standing still long enough to listen to any kind of instruction, but the kid had skill and heart. He cheered for everyone, even if they were taking his playing time. He never seemed to feel like less, even though he was the only player who was on scholarship through ULA and it was obvious all of his equipment was second-hand. Most of Park City was so filthy rich, they didn't think a thing about buying a thousand-dollar lacrosse pole, but Braden played just as well with his slightly bent stick as any of the others. It didn't hurt that Cam had taken the stick home one weekend when they had a bye week and restrung Braden's head with a new StringKing kit.

Cam almost laughed as Braden bounced in his chair. It was obvious the kid wanted to jump up and run over to give him a fist bump or something, but it looked like Miss Turner had her class under control, or maybe they were just as in awe of their gorgeous teacher as Cam was.

"*Coach* Captain Compton." Miss Turner started over, a twinkle in her dark chocolate eyes. "Welcome to our class."

"Welcome, Coach Captain Compton." The class called out, some of them giggling.

Miss Turner jumped another few notches in Cam's estimation. She could've stifled Braden's enthusiasm, but she'd validated him by adding the Coach to Cam's name.

Cam faced the class and splayed his hands. "It gets worse. My full name is Coach Captain Cameron Christian Compton."

Most of the class was laughing now.

"The best lacrosse coach in Utah." Braden called out.

"Thanks, bud. My crew calls me Quad-C when they're teasing me, but they don't know about the coach part. How do you say C to the 5th in a really great way?"

Miss Turner quirked an eyebrow. "I don't know that there is a term besides C to the 5th. Maybe we could just call you Nitro-C."

"Nitro-C?"

"The explosive fire fighter."

"Nice. I like it." What Cam really liked was her. Would it be possible for him to ask her out after a school presentation, or would that be considered unprofessional? He'd been annoyed by a girl hitting on him at a car accident a few days ago, but now he wanted to blatantly flirt with the teacher in her classroom.

Cam started his presentation about safety, and the class responded well. Miss Turner prompted them with questions. She was not only gorgeous, she was smart too. Why didn't he know her first name yet? He'd never enjoyed a presentation so much, and it was over too quickly.

After his presentation, Cam passed out stickers, plastic firefighter hats, and pencils that turned colors when they got warm. He watched Miss Turner out of the corner of his eye as she handed out the prizes to the other side of the room. He didn't know if it was deliberate that she let him go past Braden's desk, but he appreciated it.

He squatted down and held out his fist. Braden gave him a pound. "Thanks, Coach! You're the best!"

"You are, buddy." He ruffled Braden's hair and was rewarded with a huge grin. He wished he could be more involved in the little man's life, but he didn't know how to do that without making things awkward with Braden's mom. She was an attractive lady who seemed to be a little too interested in Cam, so he had to be careful.

Cam and his sister had been raised by their grandmother after their parents died, so he knew how it was to be alone and had a lot of empathy for Braden and his mom. He'd heard Braden's dad had deserted them and his mom was raising the boy by herself. She worked hard at Deer Valley resort to provide for them, but Park City wasn't a cheap place to live.

Cam finished handing out his paraphernalia, said goodbye to the class, and headed for the door. He was pleasantly surprised when Miss Turner followed him into the hallway.

She shut the door and turned to face him. "Thank you. They all ate that up. I think that may have been the first time Braden sat still for half an hour."

He chuckled. "I'm sure he's a handful, but he's a great kid. His heart is gold."

"I know. I've caught boys belittling him for being poor, and instead of being upset, he asked me not to punish them."

It ripped him up that kids would tease Braden, but he knew it probably happened. Most of these kids had no clue how hard it was to be without. Not that he'd ever struggled financially. His parents had had large life insurance policies and savings accounts that his grandma had invested for him and his sister. They'd had plenty of everything growing up. He'd been able to play lacrosse for Brighton High in Salt Lake City and never really had money concerns. When he had graduated from college and his grandma had informed him about the millions she had stashed for each of them in the bank, he and Caylee had been shocked.

"He's one of my favorite players," Cam said.

She tilted her head to the side. "I didn't peg you as a lacrosse coach."

"No?"

"Thought you'd be chopping down a forest or hunting bears on your days off from the fire station."

Cam laughed. "Ha! No. Whacking little kids with sticks in my downtime is a lot more fun."

Her eyes widened, and he laughed again. "I'm just kidding. We don't really hit them with the sticks. At least, not violently."

"Am I going to have to report you for inappropriate treatment of one of my students?"

"Who would you report me to?" Cam arched an eyebrow.

She smiled. "Guess nobody tells the Captain what to do."

"Battalion Chief and the lacrosse momma both try." He winked at her, loving the banter. "Are you going to come by the fire station so I can have JFK reimburse you for the Jeep detail? We're on Thursday and Friday this week."

"Maybe."

"Maybe you could come to Braden's game Saturday too. It's at Jeremy Ranch Elementary School."

"Maybe." She glanced back at her classroom.

Cam had to smile, but he wanted to hear a firm yes. "Can I get a better commitment than maybe?"

She bit at her lip. "I think I might be able to make those dates work."

His grin grew.

"I'd better get back in there," she said. "Make sure Braden doesn't rile up the troops."

"Wait." Cam laid his palm on her forearm.

Her eyes darted up to his. He was struck again at the depth of those dark brown eyes.

"I need to know your name."

"You know my name." She smirked at him.

"Miss Turner isn't enough. I need to know your first name."

"*Need* to know, huh?"

He nodded. It was a physical need at this point. The witty schoolteacher who'd captured him through emails was the same feisty beauty he'd been fantasizing about. Yes, he definitely needed to know her name, and he didn't want to take no for an answer.

"Hmm. I don't know. Maybe when Porky pays for my detail, I'll tell you."

"Porky?" Cam laughed hard. "Porky? Oh, Emily is going to love that one."

Miss Turner smiled and took another step into the classroom.

Cam grabbed the door above her head. "You can't just leave me without a name."

"Watch me." She strode into the classroom.

Cam watched her go, smiling to himself. He caught movement out of the corner of his eye and saw Braden waving at him again. Returning the wave, he let the door close, accepting that she'd won this round of flirtations. Maybe she'd come by the fire station. Maybe she'd come to the game Saturday. But he wasn't back on shift until Thursday, and the game wasn't any closer being on the weekend. He didn't know if he was patient enough to wait for either event.

CHAPTER FOUR

Sage pounded slowly up the trails above her cabin, south of The Canyons Ski Resort, after school on Wednesday. She loved all the trails around Park City. Her mom would've worried if she knew that Sage ran alone, but she carried a Taser with her and figured she could outrun any man or animal after she'd taken them out with that.

As much as she loved running, the hill was starting to get to her, so she distracted herself with images of Captain Compton's smile. Man, she liked him. A tough, take-charge captain who also coached a youth lacrosse team. How cool was he? She rounded a corner and tripped over something in the trail. Going down hard, she brought her hands up to break her fall. Twigs and rocks slammed against her palms, and she jarred her wrist. Rolling over with a groan, she looked back at what she'd tripped over. Her eyes widened at the black furry lump with the distinctive white stripe down the back.

"No, no, no."

The skunk seemed to glare at her with glittering, black eyes as she scooted away on her hands and heels. He whipped around, lifted his tail, and sprayed.

Sage's instinct was to scream, but luckily she turned her head instead so she didn't get a mouthful and protected her eyes. The smell was unreal. It seeped into every part of her, and she gagged several times before retching. Sadly, emptying the contents of her stomach didn't help much. The skunk gave her one more withering look then waddled away. Sage was left sitting in the rank smell.

Forcing her way to her feet, she blinked to clear her eyes and could at least thank the Lord that she didn't get any in her eyes. The smell was so bad she didn't know how she was going to get down the mountain without vomiting again.

Cam spent every spare minute of his next forty-eight hour shift watching the cameras to see if anyone was at the door and coming to visit them, especially a certain tall, blonde someone. Sadly, they didn't get any visits, and the only call the entire two days was an elderly lady who had a cold and wanted to ride in the ambulance instead of drive herself to Insta Care.

They spent the majority of their awake time training their new boot, Powers—pulling hose lines, throwing ladders, tying knots, and hoisting tools. Cam didn't know that a shift had ever dragged so long. On Friday night, the ding indicated a visitor, and he jumped to his feet and raced to the cameras.

"Expecting someone, Cap?" Emily asked.

"No. Just a boring shift."

"Agreed."

He hurried around her and looked at the cameras. Oh, no. It was the girl from the wreck last weekend. Cam turned away from the cameras and debated if he could hide out somewhere until she left.

"Cap?" JFK called out to him. "Someone here to see you." He walked into the gathering area with the girl at his side, holding a plate of cookies.

She beamed up at Cam, blushing furiously. "Hi."

"Hi." Cam nodded to her, ignoring the conspiratorial glances his crew were giving each other. "How are you feeling?"

"Great, thanks to you." She winked. "Just lots of scrapes and bruises."

Cam took the plate she held out and set it on the counter. "Thanks for the cookies. I'll walk you out."

"Smooth, Cap." JFK muttered behind them as Cam hurried toward the outer door. He wasn't trying to be smooth. He was trying not to encourage her.

He held the door open for her, and she smiled up at him. "I'm sorry if I embarrassed you with your crew when I called you hot. I just ..." She glanced down. "I'd really like to go out with you sometime."

Cam didn't know if it was possible to feel more awkward. Why had Miss Turner's subtle flirtations drawn him in while this girl's blatant come-ons just repelled him?

"I'm sorry. I don't ... You, um, me ..." Cam didn't talk a lot, but he usually had a decent command of the English language. He jammed a hand through his short hair.

"I get it. I'm not pretty enough for someone as hot as you." She glared at him and spun away.

"Wait." Cam felt like a piece of dog meat. Caylee would have his hide if he made a woman feel like she wasn't good enough. "That's not it, not at all. It's just that I'm interested in someone else."

She turned back and arched an eyebrow at him. "Okay." Her smile returned pretty quickly. "If it doesn't work out, give me a call sometime." She pulled a business card out of her purse and thrust it into his hands.

Cam forced a smile and held up the card. "Thanks."

She pranced toward her car. Cam walked back into the fire station and went to his room rather than face the jeering. It was almost nine o'clock at night, and Miss Turner still hadn't come. He'd informed JFK that he needed to have cash on hand to pay whatever the detail bill was, and for once, JFK hadn't argued with him. Of course, it might have something to do with the quiet comment he'd heard. "I hope the Hot Amazon shows." Since Cam agreed, he decided not to reprimand JFK. Unfortunately, the beautiful schoolteacher hadn't come.

Seven a.m. the next morning, he gave up looking for Miss Turner, turned everything over to A Platoon, and went home to prep for Saturday afternoon's game. Why hadn't she come? Maybe she was embarrassed to face the firefighters after parking her car illegally. But she couldn't possibly stand Braden up, could she? He'd see her today for sure. Then he'd find out her name and ask her to lunch.

He warmed his team up and prepped for the game against Sky View. He'd never been so unfocused on his team. His eyes kept wandering over to the spectator sidelines. Would she come? She'd been really cute and almost flirtatious with him. Was it too much to hope that she wanted to see him again too?

"Coach?"

His head snapped around to Braden. "Yeah?"

"Are you okay?"

"Sure. Get out there and rip some goals."

"You got it, Coach."

Braden ran out onto the field to take his place in the midfield. Cam's eyes wandered to the sidelines again, and he noticed that not only was Miss Turner not there, Braden's mom had missed another game too. He wondered if she had to work today. She did some kind of public relations for Deer Valley and seemed to work a lot of weekends. Poor kid was alone too much.

He forced himself to focus on his team and winning this game. This was just another reason why he didn't form serious relationships. At some point, they would ditch you, and he didn't need that kind of nonsense in his life right now. He didn't need that kind of nonsense in his life ever. It was better he found out that she was a flake and not interested now rather than later when he was even more captivated by her. He jerked his ball cap down lower to shade his eyes from the sun, knowing he was lying to himself. He was already fascinated by her.

CHAPTER FIVE

Almost a week had passed since the dreaded skunk attack. Sage had done the tomato bath several times, and still she could smell skunk. It was imprinted in her nasal cavities to be sure. Her class had laughed at her story, but kept commenting on how gross she smelled.

She'd missed going by Captain Compton's fire station on what she figured was his last shift, and she'd missed Braden's game. She felt horrible about that, but she couldn't go smelling like skunk.

Wednesday after school, she made the delectable brownies, sprayed herself with as much body spray as she dared, and drove to the fire station. She was almost shaking with apprehension as she pushed the doorbell. Did she still stink? Would he even want to see her? Was it going to be awkward that so much time had passed?

The door swung open, and Porky was standing there, leering at her. "Well, well, well. If it isn't Gigantor Barbie. You decided to start with brownies and see if I'd agree to go out to dinner with you? Let's see if they taste as good as you look." His nose wrinkled. "What's that smell?"

Sage's heart sank. She couldn't care less if Porky thought she was attractive, but if he could smell her, Captain Compton obviously would as well.

"The brownies aren't for you, though I would appreciate you paying for my Jeep detail."

Porky smirked at her. "Maybe after you give me a little kiss of gratitude for saving your life."

"Saving my life?"

"Cap would've killed you for parking in our way, but I always help him see the humor in the situation. So how about it, beautiful? Dinner or kiss first?"

Sage balanced the plate of brownies in one hand and yanked the bill for her Jeep detail out of her pocket with the other. She shoved it into Porky's hand. "Neither."

Porky grabbed her arm and tugged her against his chest, smashing the brownies between them.

Suddenly, he was whirled away from her. Sage took a step back, relieved to not be held by the gross, overbearing firefighter.

"Get upstairs." Captain Compton growled. "I'm going to write you up."

Porky glared at him, but he obeyed.

Sage straightened herself and looked into those impossibly blue eyes. She wished for the millionth time that she hadn't been sprayed by the skunk and could've come to see him sooner.

"Are you okay?" His deep voice washed over her with concern.

"Yes, but I don't know if the Knock You Naked Brownies survived."

His eyes widened. "Knock You Naked, huh? I'd better save them for after my shift."

"Depends how much you like your crew."

He chuckled and took a step closer. He looked too good in a firefighter t-shirt that stretched across his chest and the dark chino pants that encased his long legs. "Would you like to come in?"

"I can't, and you need to stay back." She retreated a few steps outside, away from the door. "I stink."

His nose wrinkled. "You look like you smell good."

"You can't smell me?"

"My sense of smell was partially damaged when I was eight." His gaze got much too serious, and Sage wanted to ask him what happened. "Standing that far away, you could be wearing a live skunk, and I wouldn't know or care."

"I do smell like skunk! I tripped over a skunk on a trail run, and he sprayed me full on."

"That stinks."

She laughed. "Yes, it does. It really does."

"Is that why you didn't come to see me last week or come to Braden's game?"

"Yes." She admitted, glancing down. She handed over the brownies. "I hope you enjoy them."

"I'm sure I will." His hands brushed hers as he took the plate. "Thank you."

"Thank *you* for not turning me in for parking in front of a fire hydrant."

He grinned. "No worries. I'd like to hear the full story sometime."

"Full story?" Her eyes flicked up to his.

"Why our responsible schoolteacher parked in a red zone."

"It's nothing exciting, my mom needed some tights, and I figured I could run in quickly."

"Hmm. That isn't very exciting. Do you have any more exciting stories you could share with me if we went to dinner Saturday night?"

Sage squeezed her hands together, barely withholding a squeal. "If I can't think of any, I'll make some up. My kiddos say I'm very entertaining."

"Your ... kiddos?"

"My students."

"Oh." He exhaled so loudly she could hear it. "I thought for a minute that you had children. Not that having children is a problem, but then I started worrying that you might be married, and that would be really, really bad."

"Why would that be so terrible, Captain Compton?"

"Cam." His voice was so low and appealing. "Can you please call me Cam?"

She trembled from the look he was giving her. "Why would that be so terrible, Cam?"

He smiled. "Because if you were married, I couldn't take you to dinner, now could I?"

"I guess not."

"So you've given me Knock You Naked Brownies, and you've agreed to go to dinner with me, but you still haven't told me your first name. I can't keep thinking of you as Miss Turner."

"Do you think of me then?" she asked bravely.

He licked his lips and murmured. "Only every other thought."

Sage blushed and ducked her head. Yep, he'd just said that. She wanted to cheer. "I thought guys typically have some obsession about dating the teacher. Maybe you should just keep thinking of me as Miss Turner."

"I like the idea of dating the teacher, but I'd also really like to know your name."

She just smiled at him.

"What's it going to take?"

"Let's see how good the date is Saturday night."

Cam chuckled. "All right. Where should I pick you up?"

She pulled out her phone. "What's your number?"

"435-680-4227."

Sage dialed in the number and sent him a text with her address.

"Now, I'm going to have to program you in as Miss Turner. It just feels wrong."

Sage gave him what she hoped was a flirtatious grin and backed away from him. "I'm excited for our date, and think of all the money I'm going to save on perfume."

He glanced at her kind of funny.

"Since you can't smell and all."

Cam walked her to her Jeep. He opened her door, and she slid inside. Cam bent down, his nose almost buried in her neck. Sage started, but didn't jump and thrust him away from her.

"I can smell if I get really close." He inhaled slowly, his breath brushing against her neck on the exhale. "You *do* stink like skunk."

Sage laughed shakily and placed her hands on his forearm, pushing him away from her and loving the feel of the smooth musculature under her fingertips. "I hope the skunk smell doesn't ruin the brownies."

Cam gave her an irresistible grin. "I don't think anything could ruin these brownies."

Sage knew she needed to leave now or she'd tell him her name and anything else he wanted to know. Her mom always told her men liked a little mystery. "Thanks, I'd better get going."

Cam swung her door shut, lifting the plate up as if in salute. "Thank you."

"S-sure." She stuttered out. Shifting into reverse, she spun out of there, wondering if agreeing to dinner with that man was a good idea or not.

CHAPTER SIX

Sage picked her way across the turf field by the Park City Ice Arena, the black bb-like things working their way between her bare toes. She was nervous. Why was she nervous? Glancing across the field, she saw the broad shoulders of the firefighter who she had to blame for her nerves. He gestured to one of his players and demonstrated how to pass with his stick. The boy played catch with Cam a couple of times, and Cam nodded his approval. His voice carried across the field, "Yes, Ike. That's exactly the kind of pass we're looking for."

His red neoprene shirt with Coach on the back stretched in all the right places—biceps, shoulders, and chest. He turned and spotted her. His face broke into a grin she found irresistible. Sage raised her hand in greeting. He tilted his chin up to her, all manly like, but his smile made the movement both welcoming and sexy.

Sage backed away and found herself a spot on the bleachers. The game started a few minutes later, and she really had no clue what was going on, but it was exciting to watch the boys pass, catch, run, and shoot. It looked like the defenders could hit the offense with their sticks, and several times, Sage cried out when one of the boys was knocked down.

Most of the game, she kept her eyes on the coach. Coach Captain

Cameron Christian Compton was fabulous to look at and patient with the boys—encouraging, teaching, demonstrating. She also loved that he was so into the game. He got in a very heated "discussion" with the ref after one of his boys got what sounded like a really bad penalty for pushing his mouth guard out of his mouth and playing with it with his tongue. Cam agreed that mouth guards were important, but was upset because the whistle hadn't even blown to start the play and a warning should've sufficed.

The entire exchange made Sage laugh. Cam seemed so in control, this cool firefighter leader who never got riled, but she saw he could be passionate too. He was willing to go to battle for his boys, and she thought that might be as noble as being a studly firefighter.

She figured out who Braden was, even with his helmet and gear on. He wasn't just talented. It was evident that he lived and breathed the game and loved his coach and teammates. She already knew about his lacrosse obsession from the numerous papers he'd written about the subject, but it was fun to see him in action.

At halftime, Braden's mom, Isabella, came over and sat by Sage. Isabella was an exotic-looking beauty with smooth, dark hair, and a tiny body. She was always dressed professionally and seemed like a really nice lady. Sage was grateful Braden had a loving mom. She hated that Isabella's husband had deserted both of them.

"Thanks for coming," Isabella said. "It means the world to Braden."

"He's a great kid."

"Thanks. He's got insane amounts of energy, and I'm sure he's a handful in class, but he loves you. He's always bragging about how he's got the best teacher in the world."

Sage smiled, grateful for the heartfelt praise. Braden was more work than some of the other students, but he was a great boy and obviously just needed a little more attention than his mom could give.

The game started again, and Sage really got into the action. Braden was fabulous. His teammate won the small, white ball off of, what Isabella told her, was the face off and threw it to Braden. The boy dodged around several other players, sprinted closer to the goal, and shot so fast Sage was lucky she saw the ball smack the back of the net. Cam pumped his fist in the air and yelled out. "Yes!" Next to her,

Isabella was cheering like any proud momma should be, and Sage found herself caught up in the excitement, clapping happily right along with the crowd.

The game was tied at seven, and Sage could hardly stand it. She clutched her hands together and stood, bouncing on her heels. One of Cam's boys knocked the other kid's stick, and the ball popped out. Braden swooped it off the ground and took off for the other goal.

"Go, go, go!" Sage screamed.

He shot the ball at the net, but was knocked down by a huge defender. The ball went in, but no flag was thrown. "Come on, Ref!" Sage hollered. "That was a foul!"

"Penalty," Isabella whispered to her.

"Calm down, ma'am," the ref said to her.

Sage gave a surprised laugh and held up her hands. "Come on, ref, that was definitely a fou— penalty."

"It was a legal hit." The guy informed her before running off.

Braden struggled to his feet and gave her a thumbs up. Sage returned the gesture. She glanced over at Cam. He gave her a broad smile then turned back to his boys.

Her face reddened, but a few of her fellow fans agreed that it should've been a penalty, and that made her feel a lot better. She couldn't remember ever being yelled at by a ref before. When her brother played football in high school, she'd gotten into the games and yelled and hollered, but maybe high school refs planned on being yelled at and didn't talk back to the fans. This was only little league.

"Thanks for defending my boy," Isabella said with a laugh. "Between you and Coach Compton, I think he's going to be all right."

Sage choked up a little bit. How hard it must be for this young mom to raise a rambunctious boy alone. "He has a great coach."

"Yes, he does, and whew, that man just makes my blood pressure rise." Isabella winked. "In a good way."

Sage smiled, but suddenly felt awkward. Braden's mom was interested in Cam? Why wouldn't she be? He was a good-looking, nice, hard-working guy. Did Cam return the interest? Why wouldn't he? Isabella was a gorgeous, petite, and friendly lady.

The game ended with Park City beating Syracuse 8-7, and half of the goals came from Braden.

Sage stood and stretched. She wanted to talk to Cam, so she waited while the team gave a cheer then slapped gloves with the opposing team.

Braden came tearing across the field and squeezed his mom. Sage watched them with a smile. She knew Braden had it rougher than a lot of the children in this affluent valley. It was great to see him having such huge success with lacrosse.

"I'll be right back," Isabella told her son.

"Okay." Braden gave her one more squeeze, looking into his mom's eyes and saying, "You'll be safe, right?"

Sage almost laughed at the question. His mom wasn't leaving him, but seeing the seriousness in his dark eyes made her stomach squeeze, and all thoughts of laughing dissipated.

"Of course, sweetie. Don't worry. I'm just going across the field."

"Okay. Love you."

"Love you too."

Braden released his mom and watched forlornly as she walked away.

"Hi, Braden," Sage said.

He turned and yelled out. "Miss Turner!"

"That's me." Sage waved. He ran to her, but stopped short. She always wanted to hug the boy, but there were boundaries as a teacher she had to be careful not to cross. Today, she figured it couldn't hurt. She wrapped an arm around him and gave him a squeeze. "You were amazing out there, Braden."

"Thanks, Miss Turner." His cute face lit up. "Thanks so much for coming to my game. You're the best teacher ever."

"Oh, thank you." She loved his devotion to her and hoped he didn't realize that she came to the game for his coach too. Sage glanced around for Cam, and her jaw slackened. Braden's mom was hugging him. Then she pulled back but kept a hand on his arm, and they spoke urgently to each other. They were an amazing looking couple—the well-built, good-looking firefighter and the tiny, beautiful brunette.

"Miss Turner? You okay?"

Sage focused on her student. "Yes. I just ... need to go. Good job, bud. I'll see you Monday."

"Okay!" He gave her a fist bump then dashed across the field to his mom and coach, who were still completely focused on each other. Braden ran into his mom from the side, and she was pushed into Cam again. Cam supported both of them with his arms.

Sage turned and speed-walked away. Cam and Braden's mom. It made way too much sense. They looked perfect together. Braden needed a father figure like no kid she'd ever seen, and Cam would be the ideal pick. Of course he'd be interested in a small, gorgeous woman. Who wouldn't? Sage tried to shorten her stride, feeling like everybody was watching how long her legs were. She sighed. There was no way she could hide an inch of her height.

Jumping into her Jeep, she peeled out of the parking lot. She didn't want to go out with Cam tonight and pretend he was interested in her. From what she'd just seen, she wondered if he'd even show up.

CHAPTER SEVEN

C am was on a high from his team winning this afternoon and the anticipation of taking Miss Turner to dinner. He wondered if she was adventurous. After all, she drove a Jeep with no top in April in Park City. She might be up for going to the Olympic Park and doing the zipline or alpine slide.

He texted her.

Would you be interested in going at five tonight and trying out a few activities at the Olympic Park before dinner?

The response was quick.

I'm sorry. I can't go tonight.

Disappointment rushed through him.

Okay. Maybe some other time?

We'll see.

It was a punch in the gut. He didn't chase after every woman like JFK and had little intention of ever letting anyone into his heart besides Caylee. Here he'd found himself excited about a woman and she backed out of the date with no excuse and no intention to reschedule. He should've left it alone, but he really liked her. She'd been great in every interaction they'd had, and the brownies were good enough he'd fight for a date for another taste of them. She was beautiful, fun, smart, and seemed committed to her students. Showing up at the game today and then yelling at the ref had sealed his attraction to subatomic levels.

Are you not feeling well?

Lame that he was giving her an excuse, but he kind of needed something.

No.

Cam waited, but nothing else came through. No she wasn't feeling well, or no that wasn't her excuse? His fabulous day suddenly stunk. Maybe he could go for a hike or mountain bike ride. Rain started plinking on the metal roof of his cabin, and he grimaced. Really?

He strode around his spacious living area, wondering if there was something he could work on or clean, but he'd accomplished every project imaginable, and he didn't get the place dirty enough to warrant much more than dusting, vacuuming, and an occasional deep clean.

Looking out the picturesque windows, he saw the valley was quickly darkening with the incoming storm. Spring storms could be vicious in Park City, often turning to snow. The fire station might be busy with distress calls tonight. He was tempted to call in and volunteer to run on an extra rig if the department needed him. Man, he was a lame workaholic, but there was nothing wrong with wanting to help people, right?

Striding to his mudroom, he grabbed a sweatshirt, boots, and his truck keys. He couldn't just sit here. He'd go on a drive up the mountain road behind his house for a bit and pretend he was a teenager going "digging" again. He spun out of his driveway to the road that led either down to town or up the mountain.

Bright lights streamed toward him from the direction of town. Cam waited. As the vehicle passed, he wondered if he was seeing things. But no, it was a bright red Jeep. There was a soft cover on it, but it looked exactly like Miss Turner's Jeep. That couldn't be right though. There were probably hundreds of Jeeps that looked like hers, and she was home, sick in bed, and wishing she could be going out with him, right?

Cam flipped a U-ey, gunned his engine, and followed the Jeep in his four-door Chevy truck. The paved road quickly gave way to dirt and mud. Within a few miles, they were climbing a rock strewn, one-lane road with pines encasing the road on both sides. Where could this Jeep be going? There were some older cabins up here, but not much else. The driver did a great job maneuvering the road, but it was getting treacherous. Cam considered turning back, but something about this Jeep made him want to keep following it. Going up was manageable, but he could be in trouble heading back home, and sliding off the road would be a huge issue.

The rain turned to sleet then fat drops of snow, and still the Jeep churned on. When the Jeep turned into a private driveway and parked in front of a remote cabin, Cam felt stupid. He turned in too, intent on flipping around and going home. Maybe there was an episode of Parks and Rec he hadn't watched yet.

The driver of the Jeep shot out of her door and glared at his truck like he was following her to attack her or something. Illuminated in his lights, there was no doubt. It was Sage. She sprinted to the cabin's porch without looking in his direction again.

Cam slammed his truck into park and jumped out. It was definitely the girl he wanted to be with tonight, but now he realized she'd definitely stood him up. So was she sick or not? He grunted in disgust. Who knew what her text had meant besides that she didn't want to be with him.

What on earth was she doing coming to this remote cabin in a storm? Maybe she was meeting her boyfriend here and that's why she'd told Cam she couldn't go tonight. He should've known a woman as nice, fun, and beautiful as Miss Turner was too good to be true.

CHAPTER EIGHT

Sage had considered turning back as she drove up the perilous mountain road toward her grandparents' cabin, but that dumb, huge silver truck stuck to her like peanut butter. She went from irritated to concerned to terrified. Maybe she should turn around and find a way to gun around the truck and head back down to town, but what if the guy had blocked her way, or she slid off the road? She'd always felt protected in the cabin. Her grandpa had designed a safe for guns and ammunition and taught her how to use both.

Jumping from her Jeep, she flew to the front door, unlocked it, and was inside before her pursuer exited his vehicle. She slammed the door shut, turned the deadbolt, and raced for the hiding spot above the fireplace. Removing the picture over the mantle, she fumbled with the combination the first time. *Calm down.* She took a few slow pulls of oxygen then tried the combination again. Finally, the safe sprung open and she yanked out a 1911 pistol and started sliding bullets into the chamber.

The front door vibrated with loud knocks. Sage jumped and dropped a bullet. It didn't matter, four was enough. She closed the chamber and walked on trembling legs to the front door. What if the guy was armed too? What if he shot out her windows or got inside somehow? She should've gone back to town. Dumb, dumb, dumb. But if she'd driven off the road, she would've been defenseless. She gripped the smooth metal and felt like her grandpa was here with her, watching over her.

"I've got a loaded gun and will use it if you don't leave." She shouted at the door. For effect, she racked the slide as loudly as possible.

"Miss Turner?" The person on the other side called out. "It's Cam."

Sage's body sagged with relief. Cam. He wouldn't hurt her, but why had he followed her up here? Suddenly the relief turned to concern. "What are you doing here?"

"I wanted to ask you the same thing. I thought you were sick."

Guilt made her flush. She didn't like it when people lied, and he could claim she lied to him, but she hadn't *really* said she was sick. Why did he have to follow her up here and call her on it? Why couldn't he just go be with Braden's mom, with whom he clearly belonged, and leave Sage to her miserable aloneness?

"Can I come in, please? The snow's coming from an angle now."

Sage squared her shoulders, set the gun on a side table, and opened the door. The snow was thick and driving straight from the north. Cam was getting plastered, and both of their vehicles were already covered with a layer of white.

His eyes were hooded as Sage stepped back and gestured him inside. He tried to brush off as much snow as he could then walked over the threshold. Sage shut the door behind him, nervous and wishing he wasn't here.

"I'm going to make a mess," he said.

"It's fine. Nobody comes up here but me." She glanced around the dusty old cabin with the rustic wood furniture. The soft cushions on the couch, loveseat, and chairs had been lovingly sewn by her grandmother. There were carved wooden bears as decoration and framed landscapes of the mountains and gorgeous natural settings surrounding Park City. The mantle was stacked with photos of her, her brother Levi, and their four cousins when they were much younger. The wooden floor was scratched and beaten.

Besides the open kitchen and gathering area, there were two small

bedrooms and a shared bath. It wasn't much and needed a good clean-
ing, but it had been hers for a couple of years now, and she loved it.

"Is this your cabin?" he asked.

"Yes."

"It's nice." He glanced around, but his entire body was stiff and
screamed that he wasn't any more comfortable here than she was with
him being here.

She scoffed. "It's not nice, but it's perfect for me." She turned from
him and stomped to the fireplace where wood, kindling, and matches
were stacked. Arranging the newspaper then the shards of wood, she
felt his presence next to her, but didn't look at him. He was just
commanding. Maybe she should've been concerned about having him
here, but his take-charge, built like an army tank presence wasn't scary,
at least not in a way that he would hurt her. It was scarier that she was
so attracted to him and couldn't act on that.

He helped her lift some logs onto the pile of kindling and then sat
back while she lit the match and touched it to the rolled newspaper. It
caught, and within seconds, a nice blaze was rolling and heat soon
followed. The power was on, but who knew what would happen in a
storm like this, and she needed something to do with him staring at
her like he was.

"I can't believe the captain let the helpless female actually light
the fire."

His eyebrows arched. "I'm only in charge at the station, on a call,
or on the lacrosse field. You can be in charge in your cabin."

She smirked at him, not believing him for a second. "I don't think
there's any situation where you aren't in charge."

The snow was melting in his hair, and a few drops ran down the
side of his face. Sage couldn't resist brushing them off. The bristly
growth on his cheeks enraptured her, and she kept her fingers there for
longer than she should have. "Mountain Man," she whispered.

Cam smiled and then captured her hand with his own. It was
much too intimate, kneeling next to the fire with the storm obliter-
ating any outside light and this good-looking man staring at her so
intently.

Sage stood and broke from his grasp. She flipped on the overhead light, hurried to one of the armchairs and sat. "Why did you follow me?"

Cam climbed to his feet and sank into the couch. "I was going for a drive and saw your Jeep. I couldn't believe it was you." He pinned her with a look. "Since you're sick and all. So I followed you to make sure you were okay."

"I'm feeling much better now." Sage blinked and looked away, embarrassed that she hadn't been brave enough to tell him why she didn't go and now he was calling her on it.

Cam grunted. "Glad to hear it." He glanced everywhere but at her then finally muttered. "I still don't even know your first name."

"It's Sage." She'd forgotten he didn't know it. All the flirtatiousness and teasing about her name was gone. She didn't know why he even cared that he didn't know her name. Man, oh, man, she had flubbed this one up.

Sage stood and rushed to the window. White flakes were coming down in increasing intensity. She couldn't even see their vehicles or the sun, though it was hours from sunset. "Spring storm, who knew?"

"These can be vicious."

Cam joined her at the window. He smelled clean and manly with a slight hint of warm musk. Why did he have to smell so good?

"I hate to impose on your hospitality," he said.

Sage winced. It was obvious he really didn't want to impose. He was probably ticked at her for ditching their date and not giving any reason, and she didn't blame him. Yet how could she tell him she'd been jealous of her student's mom and was afraid he was interested in Isabella because she was short and beautiful.

"But I don't know that I can drive safely out of here."

She nodded. He was probably right. "You're welcome to stay until the storm passes."

"Thanks." He looked around. "Are you prepared for a storm?"

"Yes." Was she prepared? This was her wilderness survival cabin. Grandpa had made sure they could survive the apocalypse up here. "I have food, water, and plenty of firewood. We can start the generator if the storm knocks the electricity out and we need more heat than the fire."

"I'm sure the electricity will be fine."

Oh, man, this felt stiff and uncomfortable. She shouldn't have backed out of their date without explaining, but how did she defend an irrational jealousy of a woman who seemed like the right fit for Cam?

Cam returned to the couch and settled in. "Looks like we have some time on our hands. Do you want to tell me why you backed out of our date?"

Sage wished he hadn't gone there. What happened to the reclusive captain who kept everything close and guarded? She wanted that guy back.

"Um ... no?"

"No?" His eyebrows arched up again. Sage realized for probably the twentieth time that his face was very attractive to her. Especially with the sexy scruff that was coming in a dark reddish brown. Yummy.

She crossed the distance and held out her hand. "I think you'd better take that sweatshirt off and let it dry."

Cam eyed her, but complied, pulling the sweatshirt up and over his head. As he did so, his t-shirt caught and rode up with the sweatshirt, revealing a sculpted abdomen and chest that made her mouth go dry. She couldn't help but notice the scars on his abdomen that looked like they continued around to his back.

Reaching out, she touched the bumpy skin. Cam drew back and tugged his t-shirt into place.

"What happened?" she whispered.

Cam stood and draped his sweatshirt over one of the chairs closest to the fire. The room was warming considerably, but not nearly enough heat to explain why his face was darkening to red.

"Occupational hazard." His voice was barely audible.

"Oh." It looked like he'd been burned badly. You'd think he would want to stay as far away from fire as possible. Yet he didn't just keep fighting fires, he'd worked his way up to captain. Impressive, but she wondered about the scars he was hiding. With the suits firefighters wore, how would fire have gotten through those layers to burn his abdomen so horribly?

"Are you hungry? I can make us something to eat." She bustled into the kitchen.

"Yeah, I was planning on taking a beautiful lady to dinner."

Sage bristled. Was he going to be throwing that out into the awkward space between them all night? How long before the storm broke and he could leave? She just wanted to enjoy some peace and quiet before she went back to school on Monday.

"I'm sorry, okay!" She whipped around to face him. "I shouldn't have responded vaguely and let you think I was sick."

Cam walked toward her, and she found herself backing slowly up. He kept coming, the look on his face determined and much too intriguing.

Sage backed into the pantry and was left with no escape route. Cam stopped in front of her. He was at least four inches taller than her, and she liked that a lot. What she didn't like was the look in his eyes, uncertain and exposed. She'd hurt him, and she had no way to explain.

"Why?" he asked simply.

"Why did I lie?"

"Why didn't you want to go out with me?"

Sage could feel how much the words cost him. He definitely wasn't a guy that was in touch with his inner feelings, and he'd just made himself vulnerable to a woman who had already hurt him. How to explain without looking like an idiot or hurting him worse?

"Um, I didn't think I should."

He simply stared at her.

"Because of Isabella." It rushed out before good sense could stop her.

"Isa ... who?" His brow furrowed.

Sage looked down, completely confused. "Braden's mom. I saw you hugging her at the game. I thought you two were together, and it isn't fair for me to get in the middle of that, and besides, Braden really needs a dad."

Cam glowered down at her, and any further explanation caught in her throat.

"If you didn't want to go with me, it's fine." He bit out. "But you don't need to keep piling lies on."

"I'm not lying." Sage straightened up. "I never lie."

He guffawed.

"Okay, so I misled you about *possibly* being sick, but I did see you hugging Isabella. I'm sure you understand how much Braden needs a dad. He and Isabella deserve someone great." She wanted to say, *someone like you*, but it was implied, right? "How could I get in the way of their happiness? I love that kid."

Cam stepped back and stared at her like she was insane. "I love the kid too, but I have no desire to date his mom, let alone marry her." He said the word like it was sour milk on his tongue.

Sage felt happier than she had in hours. Even though it was a guilty pleasure, putting her happiness before someone else's. "You aren't interested in Isabella?"

"No. Why would you even think that?"

"She said something that made me think ..." She didn't want to make Isabella embarrassed if she found out Sage shared her comment about Cam making her blood pressure rise. "And like I said, I saw you hugging her after the game."

"Is that why you took off without saying hi?"

She nodded.

Cam gazed down at her. "Are you slow or something?"

"Excuse *me*." How dare he? She'd graduated at the top of her class, thank you very much.

"Have you looked in a mirror lately? Do you even realize how gorgeous you are?"

Heat flushed into her face. "Braden's mom is every bit as pretty as me, and she's a sweetheart, and she's vulnerable and needs someone, and she's ..." She looked down and finally forced out the descriptor that she could never aspire to. "Petite."

Cam took that step closer again, planted his hands on each side of her head, and leaned in. Oh, my, goodness! She was going to hyperventilate from the nearness of his body, the smell of his musky cologne, and the searing look in his eyes.

"I've never seen a woman as beautiful as you." He paused as if to let that sink in, but then he continued. "I don't care if you're over six feet tall, and I really like that you're feisty."

A great compliment and a slap to the face at the same time. He thought she was gargantuan. How could he claim she was over six feet? She was a full half-centimeter shy of six feet. Jerk. And he definitely didn't think she was a sweetheart. She didn't want to be feisty. Ugh.

Slipping under his arms, Sage took a steadying breath. "I'm going to run get the groceries from my car."

Cam stopped her with a hand on her arm. The simple touch was nice, too nice. He'd said he *didn't* care if she was over six feet. It wasn't *exactly* a slam. She shook her head. Yes, it was. She'd been teased her whole life for being an Amazon woman, reaching five-nine in the seventh grade, but not stopping there. She'd been taller than most of the boys until sophomore year of high school. Even then, only a handful were taller and ever asked her out. It still stung, and she hated that she was so touchy, but that was life for a colossal woman.

"I'll grab them," he said. "Is your car unlocked?"

She nodded and watched him stomp from the cabin, slamming the door behind him. Sinking into a chair, she banged her head against the wooden table. He'd offended her, and then she'd ticked him off. How in the world were they going to co-exist in this cabin until the storm broke? What if he had to stay the night? At least there were two bedrooms and she'd brought up the fresh sheets and towels.

Cam slammed back into the cabin. His face was an unreadable mask, and Sage wished they could start all over. She'd really liked him before. He set the bags full of groceries on the counter and headed back outside without saying anything to her.

Sage unloaded the groceries into the fridge and decided she was going to make her chicken enchiladas tonight instead of saving them for dinner tomorrow. She didn't know why she cared if she impressed Cam with her cooking, but maybe it would help restore his good opinion about her.

Flipping the light on in the kitchen, she pulled out the chicken, a frying pan, and the olive oil. Cam stomped back in and shut the door behind him, his arms full of the laundry basket with the clean laundry and another bag of groceries. He set the laundry basket down and then walked to her side with the groceries.

"Can I help you in here?"

"Um, I think I've got it." His presence almost overwhelmed her. He was just so good-looking, appealing, and take-charge. She wanted to bow and say, "O Captain, My Captain" or something. Gritting her teeth, she vowed to never say that. "You can relax by the fire. Dinner will take about an hour."

"I can't relax while you work. How about I put the clean bedding on. Then I'll help you in here." It wasn't a request, more like a command.

Sage froze with cold chicken in one hand and the shears in the other. "You think we'll need both beds?" Her voice squeaked.

He nodded, his eyes sweeping over her face. "Unless you want to share?"

Her eyes widened, and her hands trembled. She hadn't meant *that*. She'd been hoping that the storm would blow over and he wouldn't be staying.

"I'm teasing," he said in a husky voice that didn't help the situation at all. "Do you want me to sleep in my truck?"

"Don't be silly."

"I don't think I'm the one who's being silly here." He stared at her with a look of longing and apprehension.

Sage didn't know if she wanted to fire back at him for calling her silly, or reassure him that she wanted him here. But she really *didn't* want him sleeping in here with her. Even if it was in a separate room. Just the act of sleeping in the same cabin felt too intimate, and she did not need intimate with a man who confused her and thought she was too tall and feisty. Instead of responding, she turned back to the pan and continued cutting up chicken into the sizzling oil.

Cam exhaled loudly. He turned away from her, picked up the laundry basket, and headed to her bedroom first. Both beds were queens, so it didn't really matter which set of sheets he put on which bed, but it kind of bugged her. She liked the flannel sheets better, and she didn't like him being in her personal space—teasing her, complimenting her, and belittling her. This was her retreat. Her cabin. She took fabulous care of twenty-three nine and ten-year-olds five days a week. She loved her kiddos and her job, but sometimes she just needed peace and quiet. Was it too much to ask she have a break from people once in a while? Especially a certain hot fireman who excited, frustrated, and confused her.

She finished the chicken, washed her hands, started slamming cans onto the counter, and then proceeded to hack up the avocado, green onion, and cilantro. This guacamole would be smooth. That was for sure.

Cam was suddenly by her side again. "What did that onion ever do to you?" he asked, but there was no smile in his voice or on his face.

"Intruded on my space without being invited." She flung back at him.

Cam's eyebrows arched up, and his lips twitched in what might have been a smile. "How can I help in here?"

"Stir the chicken." She commanded. "Then open up all those cans, containers, and the bag of cheese, and put them in the mixing bowl."

He saluted her. "Got it, Cap."

"Don't call me Cap." Man, she was annoyed with him, but even more annoyed with herself. She didn't want him here, yet she found herself wanting to smile at him instead of glower, and she really liked looking at him. How shallow was she?

"What should I call you?"

"Miss Turner will be just fine."

He shook his head and stirred the chicken with a sigh. "And just like that, I lose first name privileges."

"You're going to lose a lot more than that if you keep teasing me." She held up the knife threateningly.

Cam's hand was around her wrist before she could move. He lightly grasped it and smirked at her. "You shouldn't threaten. You'd never hurt someone. The sweet little teacher doesn't have it in her."

Sage pulled her hand free, turned back to her guacamole and muttered. "Not sweet and you already confirmed I'm not little."

Cam stared at her, but didn't say anything. Sage sighed and seasoned the guacamole with garlic, sea salt, and lime juice. It was going to be a very long night.

Cam wasn't sure how he kept offending her. He told her she was the most beautiful woman he'd ever seen, and she got all ticked off. Maybe it was him coming onto her that ticked her off. He'd been uncomfortable when that girl from the car wreck had hit on him. Sage must be feeling something similar with him. He had to control himself when that impulse to touch her got strong. She couldn't possibly be interested in him—lying that she was sick so she could avoid their date and then making up that lame excuse that he should be dating Braden's mom because Braden needed a dad and Isabella was petite. He was almost six-five. Why would he want a short girl? Crazy woman anyway.

They worked silently to make dinner, and he did a pretty good job of avoiding staring at her beautiful face or her lean frame in her fitted, long-sleeved, blue running shirt and black tights. Didn't women know what they did to men when they wore those things? If she had any idea how attracted he was to her, she'd force him to sleep in his truck.

Finally, the food and dishes were on the table, and they sat down. Cam didn't consider himself a talkative person, but he couldn't handle this tense silence much longer. There was always background noise at the fire station, either the television or music. Even an annoying talk radio guy who thought he knew it all would be better than this.

Sage looked at him as they sat across from each other at the oak butcher block table. "Do you want to pray?" she asked.

"I'd love to." He bowed his head and thanked the Lord for Sage, her hospitality, and the food and prayed that they could be safe from the storm.

She uttered amen, and the mood seemed to lighten a little bit. Cam gestured for her to dish up first. She sighed and scooped a large serving of the chicken enchiladas onto her plate. "Always the gentleman, eh, Cap?"

"My grandmother raised me to be," he said before he realized the follow-up question was inevitable.

"Your grandmother raised you?" She dipped a chip into her guacamole, placed some in her mouth and watched him as she chewed delicately.

Cam glanced down at his plate, toying with his pile of enchilada. It looked and smelled almost as great as Sage, when he'd gotten close enough to her a few times to catch her scent with his damaged senses. But until he deflected her question, he'd take no satisfaction in the food.

"Yeah. She was a great lady."

"Was?" Her eyes were so full of compassion. He usually hated that look, but on her beautiful face it wasn't as bad as usual.

"She and my grandfather have both been gone a couple of years."

"I'm sorry." She took a sip of her milk and admitted. "My grandparents have been gone for a few years too. Both sets. It sucks."

Cam smiled at her terminology even though it was nothing to smile about. "It does." He commiserated. "I never knew my dad's parents, but my mom's were"— His voice caught —"The best."

"What about the rest of your family?" she asked softly.

"It's just me and my younger sister, Caylee, now." Cam shook his head. He didn't delve into this kind of conversation with anyone. He gestured to the food. "You should eat while it's warm."

"So should you."

He nodded and made an effort, placing a bite of enchilada in his mouth. It was a great mix of creamy, spicy, and warm. "It's really good," he said.

"Thank you."

They ate quietly for a few minutes, but it wasn't as uncomfortable or cold as before. Cam enjoyed the enchiladas, freezer corn, chips, guacamole, and freshly-canned salsa. He hadn't had freezer corn or home-canned salsa since Grams died.

"Do you have a garden?" he asked.

She shook her head. "No. My mom rocks the soil though, and as long as I pull a weed on occasion and help her harvest, she gives me more bottled food than I can use."

He could just envision a large family home with a huge garden and Sage with a woman who was older, but looked like her, laughing and talking as they dug in the dirt. He felt a longing for a mom he hadn't allowed himself in years. Shoving in a large bite of enchilada, he chewed and swallowed quickly.

"You okay?" Sage asked.

"Yeah, sure." He didn't say anything else as they finished their dinner, and thankfully, she didn't ask. Standing as soon as his plate was clear, he started gathering dishes.

Sage stood, but he gestured her back down. "You cooked, so I have to clean up."

"What?"

"Firehouse rules."

"Really?"

He actually did smile. "No. Powers, he's the new guy, the Boot, does most of the cleanup, but we help sometimes and everyone takes turns cooking."

Sage stood next to him, despite his protests, and they quickly cleaned up the table, put food away, and did the dishes. Cam liked it a lot. They were comfortable together, and hopefully, she'd forgiven him for whatever he'd done to tick her off earlier.

"Do you like to cook?" she asked him.

"I don't love it, but I can follow a recipe okay."

She regarded him. "No imagination in your cooking though?"

He shook his head. "I follow the rules."

They were side by side as she washed dishes and he rinsed. She bumped against his shoulder. "You always follow the rules?"

Cam looked down at her and thought if he had to break some rules to kiss her, he would definitely do it. But he had to tell her the truth and remind himself that she probably wasn't interested in kissing him. "Yes, always."

She licked her lips and looked him up and down. "Hmm. We might have to teach you how to bend them."

He held onto a slippery plate and wondered if she was blatantly flirting with him or if it was just a really good dream.

"At least where cooking is concerned. Food tastes better when a recipe isn't followed so rigidly."

He smiled, stacked the clean plate, and took another soapy one from the pile. "Hmm. If everything you cook tastes as good as tonight's food, I might be convinced."

Sage winked. "I make everything taste delectable."

"I bet you do." Cam smiled happily, liking her flirtatious side. Maybe this night was going to turn into something good. He was suddenly very grateful that he'd followed her and that they were effectively being snowed in. If they spent a few days up here together, who knew where it would lead?

CHAPTER NINE

Sage enjoyed the evening with Cam. They played cards, ate some of her candy stash, and talked easily while the snow piled up in the windowsills. Obviously Mother Nature had forgotten it was spring and decided to retreat to winter.

The conversation with Cam was nothing serious. She still didn't know why his grandparents had raised him or how he really got the scars on his abdomen, but he'd told her a little about his sister, Caylee, who was going to school at Pepperdine University in California and was his favorite person in the world. He'd also told her about his crew at the fire station and playing lacrosse in high school and on the University of Utah's club team in college.

It'd been a good night, and she was glad he was here with her. When she turned down her bed and realized he'd made up hers with the flannel sheets, she sighed and burrowed in happily. She lay there drowsily, listening to the wind howl outside and feeling safe with the burly firefighter in the room next to hers.

She'd barely fallen asleep when a loud yell yanked her awake. Sitting up in bed, she was disoriented for a few seconds until she remembered she was at her cabin. But who had yelled, and where was her gun? Dang.

She'd left it on the entryway table. Had Cam yelled? Had someone broken in? She'd been so enraptured with Cam and secure in her winter wonderland, she hadn't even checked the lock on the front door.

Sliding her feet onto the floor, she grimaced at the cold wood.

"No!" Cam's voice was unmistakable from the next room.

Sage crept out of her room, glancing at the front door, but everything was quiet and Cam's door was closed. Slowly, she crossed to his door and eased it open. He was writhing on the bed, his frame so large he made the queen mattress look small.

"Cam?" She squeaked out.

His head shook back and forth as he muttered. "No, no!"

Sage crept close to the bed and stretched across the mattress to gently grasp his shoulder. "Cam," she said a little bit louder.

"No! Sage!" His yell was full of anguish and fear. He grabbed Sage's arm and yanked her onto the mattress.

"Cam!" She cried out, banging into his side. "Stop!"

His eyes flew open, and he sat up quickly, pulling her against his bare chest. "Sage? Are you okay?"

"I'm fine." She shook her head. "It's you I'm worried about." She'd never had vivid or terrifying nightmares, but she'd heard they could really affect a person.

Cam released a ragged breath and cradled her in his arms. "Oh, thank you, Lord." He rasped out.

Sage didn't know how to react. She was encircled by his warmth and strength, but she wasn't sure if he really wanted her here, or was just upset from whatever nightmare he'd been having. He'd said her name, so he must know it was her, but for some reason, she felt like he didn't realize he was holding her, like he thought she was someone else. She'd awakened from dreams confused before, mad at someone for no reason, or thinking she'd kissed her grisly old neighbor or something crazy.

She glanced up, the outline of his face barely discernible in the darkened room. "Cam, are you sure you're okay?"

He rocked her gently back and forth, his arms tightening around her. "I am now. I was so scared, Sage. The fire was out of control, and I could see you—" He broke off and exhaled. "It was just a dream, just a dream."

She didn't know if he was talking to her or himself. He was dreaming about her? Did that mean anything to her, to them?

"But you're okay, and I've got you now." Cam wrapped his palm around her cheek, tilted her face, and kissed her before she could even think about a response.

Sage quickly got lost in the kiss. Cam's commanding presence in everything he did definitely extended to his kissing abilities. He took control, but she wasn't about to complain. His mouth was warm and pleasure receptors were firing everywhere from her lips to wherever his hands touched. She wrapped her arms around his bare back and held on, savoring the feel of his developed muscles under her fingertips.

Cam released her from the kiss and simply held her close. "Oh, Sage."

Sage was confused and pretty sure Cam was going to regret his breakdown in the light of day. She pulled back and stared at him. "Cam. What's going on? Are you sure you're okay?"

He blinked a couple of times, and then his arms fell away. He swallowed hard and scooted away from her, banging his back on the headboard. "I apologize." He blew out a long breath. "I ... have pretty bad dreams sometimes, and I got confused. Please forgive me."

As the warmth of his arms and the fire of his kiss dissipated, she was left with nothing but his regret. She pushed off the bed and stood. "No worries. Glad you're okay."

"Thanks."

Sage padded across the wood floor. She glanced back from the entrance to his room. He was in the shadows, so all she could see was his large frame and his arms folded tightly across his muscular chest. He didn't say anything, and she had no clue how she was supposed to react to all of this. Shutting his door carefully behind her, she hurried back to her bed and slipped into the soft sheets. All she could think about was Cam holding her. He'd been confused and disoriented, kissing her on impulse.

What was her excuse?

CHAPTER TEN

C am woke to the sun breaking through the clouds and the smell of bacon and cinnamon that even his damaged senses could appreciate. He'd slept later than he normally would, but that nightmare had flipped him out. He couldn't go to bed for hours after seeing Sage's beautiful face in the flames, her calling out to him. No matter how hard he ran, he couldn't reach her.

Sage. He brushed his hand over his rough cheeks. He'd grabbed her and kissed her last night. The kiss had been better than anything he could dream up. He'd been so relieved that she was okay, that it was all a nightmare, kissing her had seemed like the perfect reaction, and he loved the way she'd returned it. Still, he shouldn't have done it. There was no excuse for him reacting so impulsively. He was Captain Compton. Always in control of the situation. He'd definitely failed at that last night.

He slipped on his t-shirt, jeans, socks, and shoes then stripped the bed. He put the sheets in the laundry basket and folded the blankets and stacked them on the bed with the pillows, leaving them the same way he'd found them earlier when he had made up the beds. Since the sun was out, he definitely wasn't going to be staying another night. He shouldn't feel so depressed at the thought. He'd come here uninvited and definitely shouldn't overstay a welcome that had never been there.

He eased out of his room and into the bathroom. He felt awkward taking a shower, and he didn't have clean clothes anyway, so he just washed up the best he could then decided to brave facing Sage.

She was wearing a gray fitted shirt and patterned blue and burgundy running pants today. Facing away from him as she flipped something on the griddle, Cam was able to unabashedly admire the lean lines of her body and her smooth, blonde hair cascading down her back. Was it really fair to the rest of the female population for one woman to be that beautiful?

Turning, she spotted him. Her smile was definitely forced, and he knew he'd ruined things between them yet again.

"Morning lazy bones," she said. "Hungry?"

"Always." He gave her a smile that probably wasn't any more genuine than the one on her face. "Can I help?"

She shook her head quickly. "No, just sit."

The table already had juice, bacon, cut up strawberries and bananas, butter, and syrup set out. Cam wished he'd woken up earlier so he could help her, but there was nothing he could do about it now. He sat and glanced out the windows, admiring the picturesque view. The snow decorated the deep green pines and sparkled in the rising sun. There were still some low gray clouds hanging around after the storm that gave an amazing contrast.

Sage stepped up next to him and set down a plate of French toast. The sweet cinnamon scent wasn't as intriguing as the pear perfume he'd come to associate with her the few times he'd been close enough to really smell her.

Her eyes followed where he'd been looking. "Isn't it pretty outside?"

He focused on her face. "The most beautiful thing I've ever seen."

She turned and saw his gaze was on her. Her cheeks went pink. She quickly sat and said, "I'm praying" before offering a short prayer.

Cam filled his plate and enjoyed the delicious food. "Thank you for feeding me again. I'll cook for you next."

She smiled. "I'd like that."

Cam took a drink of juice, thinking maybe there was a chance to have a relationship with Sage and maybe get a real kiss sometime, not a stolen in the night, half-awake kiss. Though he didn't mind that one at all.

"What are you thinking?" she asked.

Cam straightened, unnerved by the question and not at all ready to tell her he'd been thinking about how he grabbed her and kissed her last night. Was she mad at him for taking advantage of her vulnerability? He'd gotten the impression she wanted to be in his arms, but maybe he'd read her all wrong.

"Um, this food's really good." He took another bite of French toast and then polished off his bacon to prove his point. "Do you cook like this for yourself all the time? Most women I know wouldn't dream of eating bacon." A woman who had bacon on hand when she wasn't planning on anyone else being there but her? He liked it.

"Yes. I like fatty breakfast meats." Her answer was stiff.

How had he possibly offended her now? Eating bacon was somehow wrong? Sage stood and started carrying leftovers to the counter.

Cam shoved down the rest of his French toast and followed her, helping her clear the table, put food away, and wash the dishes. Unlike last night, there was no feeling of camaraderie as they worked. It was like the crew he'd worked on where two of the guys hated each other, and the whole station just felt cold all the time.

Cam kept racking his brain. Was she mad about the kiss still, or had he said something wrong? This was just another reason why he didn't go on more than a date or two with the same woman. Who knew what in the world they were thinking?

With the dishes finished, Cam didn't know what to do with his hands or his mouth. Neither had been a great help in the past twenty-four hours.

Sage was avoiding his eyes. Cam got the feeling she was ready for him to go. Probably past ready. He glanced outside again. "Well, the storm's broken. Guess it's safe for me to drive home."

"Guess so." She walked toward the front door.

Ouch. Definitely more than ready to shut the door behind his backside. "Are you going to be okay up here by yourself?" he asked.

She turned to face him, and her eyes flashed and darkened at the same time. He loved that deep brown color. "I come up here several times a month all by my lonesome. I don't need a big, tough firefighter protecting me."

Cam's eyes widened, but he thought it was best he left that one alone. He followed her to the door. "Do you explore the trails?"

"Yes, and I have pepper spray, a Taser, and a gun." She pointed to the entry table. "Don't worry about me."

"Okay, good." Now he was in trouble for trying to be a gentleman. "Well, thank you for everything."

She nodded.

Cam swung the door open. The air was chilly but not freezing. The snow was already melting and dripping off the roof and their vehicles. "Bye," he said and walked out onto the porch.

She shut the door behind him without a response.

"Touchy female," he said under his breath. He hadn't even reached his truck when the cool breeze on his bare arms reminded him he'd left his sweatshirt hanging on a chair by the fire. His sister had given it to him for Christmas. He felt bad writing off a present, especially one from Caylee, but he wasn't going back in there to get it.

CHAPTER ELEVEN

The next week was busy with school and helping her mom clean out the yard for the spring. Sage had started a very disturbing habit of sleeping with the sweatshirt Cam had left at her cabin. It ticked her off, but every night she found herself curled around his soft Under Armour sweatshirt. Sadly, his musky cologne wore off after night three. She tried multiple times to decide if things went right or wrong with them last Saturday night. She'd taken offense a few times, but had he really intended it? Saying she was six feet tall, well, she was close, and asking if she cooked like this all the time and that most women didn't eat bacon didn't necessarily mean he thought she overate and was too big. She was a bigger girl. Her aunt who didn't have a filter on her mouth had always told her that. "You're just big boned. It's all right. Wear it well." She definitely was taller than, and probably outweighed, most men, but she was active and ate reasonably and thought she looked fine.

Her phone rang Friday at about six as she drove home from slaving in her mom's yard. She was tired and ready to soak in the tub, make a quick pasta dinner, and go to bed. The screen showed a Facetime call from her brother, Levi. Yes! Her smile was genuine as she tapped on the screen. "Hey, big brother. How's the desert treating you?"

"It's miserable. Enough about me. What's new in your life?"

She laughed. He never wanted to talk about himself or his medical practice on Bagram Air Base in Afghanistan. It was actually pretty sad that whatever he was doing was so miserable or hard that he didn't share it with her, but the way he always said, "Enough about me" never failed to make her laugh since he rarely talked about himself.

"Nothing exciting. Helping Mom get the yard in shape and get the garden plot ready."

"That definitely isn't anything exciting. You haven't talked them into selling that old place yet?"

Sage smiled, knowing Levi loved their "Homestead" as their dad called it as much as she did. Their parents had several acres of yard and garden, and though it was a lot of work, it was worth it.

"Dad doing okay? He keeps lying to me."

Sage parked her Jeep in the driveway of her little house and climbed out, glad she could focus on Levi's face now she wasn't driving. He'd been teased his whole life about being a pretty boy with his flowing blond hair, regal features, and bright blue eyes. He looked like the Prince Charming dolls she used to play with. Most people said the two of them looked a lot alike, though he was one of the few men who made her feel small. She sighed. Cam had made her feel small and feminine until he opened his mouth. If only they could've kept kissing and forgot about verbal communication.

"Dad's doing pretty well. Frustrated that the docs can't cure him and he can't help mom more, but he doesn't seem to be in as much pain with this new medication he's taking." Their dad had suffered from severe fibromyalgia for two years now. A retired contractor, he hated not being able to work and move like he used to.

"There's something weird going on with you right now, sis."

Sage pushed away from her Jeep and cringed. She turned the camera from her face. "What are you talking about?"

"I don't want to see your Jeep, I want to see you."

Sage sighed and lifted the phone back up. "Happy?"

"Yes, my beautiful little sister."

"We both know I'm not little."

"Stop that crap, sis. You're perfect. Every man thinks so. Believe me, I've heard about it far too much."

"Thanks, Levi. I just …" She licked her lips. "I met someone I really like, but he made a few comments about me being tall and about me eating a lot."

"Whoa. Do I need to kick his trash or what?"

Sage laughed. If Levi had been in the country, he might be the only man she knew who was tough enough to take Cam on, though Cam was thicker. She liked all of Cam's muscles, maybe a little too much. "No. I don't *think* he meant anything by it."

"I don't want to say you're too sensitive about your height."

"But I am?" She squinted against the bright sun and headed for the porch so she could see Levi better.

"Maybe. Why does it bug you, sis?"

"You don't know how it is." She sat in her porch swing. "It's cool for a man to be tall."

He sighed. "If only you'd listen to me. You're beautiful, Sage, and there's nothing wrong with a woman being tall. If you knew how many times I had to thrash somebody in high school because they were going on about how 'hot' you were, you'd believe me."

Sage smiled. Levi had always been her cheerleader. She could still hear his whoops and loud clapping across the football field when she'd been crowned Homecoming Queen. She never told him about her first attendant whispering, "Sorry the football captain is a foot shorter than you." He wasn't quite a foot, but she had thrown the pictures away.

"So you like this guy?"

"What if I do?" She loved to tease Levi.

"Then you'd better wait until I get home in two months so I can give my approval."

"Don't worry. Nothing's going to happen in two months."

"A lot can happen in two months, sis."

His words were too serious and so was the look on his face. Sage lived in constant fear that a lot could happen to him in two months. Even if he wasn't in physical danger, he'd already changed more than she could've imagined. She knew he saw a lot of sad things with both the military personnel he treated and the locals. He'd become more hardened and less happy than she ever thought her brother could be. If this last two months could just be over and done. He could retire if he wanted, start a private practice. Maybe someday, he'd be the carefree, fun brother she used to know. But then again, maybe not. Sometimes life just took the happy out of a person.

"So tell me more about this guy."

"Like what?" She rocked on the porch swing, and her thoughts fell to that kiss last Saturday night. Cam's huge pec muscles brushing against her. Her hands exploring the musculature of his back. What *had* he been wearing? Not much.

"His name for one."

"Oh." She started guiltily. Levi would be ticked if he knew everything that had happened Saturday night. "He's Coach Captain Cameron Christian Compton."

"Whoa." Levi chuckled. "Did his parents not like him?"

"I don't think he has any parents." She wished she knew more about Cam.

"Oh, that sucks. So a captain and a coach? Of what?"

"Firefighting and lacrosse."

"Hmm. Maybe I could learn to like him. Though football would be better."

"Of course it would." She laughed at his football obsession. "I went to a game though and it was pretty fun."

"They're faster paced than football, I'll give them that."

She shook her head. "Yeah. Well, we'll see if you even meet him. Doubt I'll remember his name in two months." She grinned, knowing she wouldn't forget Cam even if she never saw him again.

"With a name that long I wouldn't blame you. When do you see him next?"

Sage appreciated that Levi wanted to be involved in her life, but sometimes it got to be a bit much. He liked to push her out of her comfortable spots. "Not sure."

"Why not?"

"I wasn't too nice to him when he left the cabin Sunday morning."

"Sunday morning! What the—"

Sage winced at the expletive Levi used. "Levi!"

"What are you doing having him stay at your cabin? I swear I will come home and kick both your butts."

"Nothing happened." She hastened to reassure him. "He followed me to the cabin, but there was a storm, and I couldn't just toss him out in the snow."

"Yes, you could have."

"Levi! We slept in separate rooms. We didn't even ... do anything." She finished lamely, not looking at the camera.

"What was that pause?"

"What pause?" She picked at some peeling paint on her porch swing. She'd need to repaint it this summer.

"You definitely paused."

"Oh, my, goodness, you are such an older brother!"

"Yes, I am. What did you do? Spill it now." He glowered at her, and for the first time she was very glad for the seven-thousand, four-hundred, and twenty-nine miles between them.

"I'm hanging up now." She informed him.

"Don't you dare. Two months will come fast, and then I'll—" His brow furrowed as he thought.

"You'll what?" She taunted, tossing her ponytail and batting her eyelashes. It wasn't smart to goad him. Levi could be vicious with pranks and retribution. But he wasn't here now. There was nothing he could do to her.

"I'll put your Jeep up on blocks and give your tires away."

She gasped. "You wouldn't."

"Try me, and if you hang up on me, I'll call Dad immediately."

"You are such a child!" She shouted. Her neighbor was out watering her begonias, and she peeked over the fence at Sage. "Sorry." Sage called out to her. "Dealing with my brother."

Mrs. Toolson smiled and waved. "Tell that handsome hunk hello from me."

"Mrs. Toolson thinks you're a handsome hunk."

Levi's loud laugh grated on her nerves. "She would. Tell her hello."

"He says hello back." Sage called out.

Mrs. Toolson grinned and tottered off.

"Details of whatever happened Saturday night. Now!" Levi insisted, the smile gone from his face.

Sage sighed. "It wasn't a big deal. He had a nightmare, and I went to wake him up." Wow, this story sounded lame in the light of day. "He kissed me."

Levi's lips thinned, but he didn't respond.

"He must've regretted it immediately. He apologized and acted all weird and formal with me."

"And you kicked him out the next morning and haven't seen him since."

"Pretty much sums it up."

He sighed. "You like him."

"Yeah."

"I hate to say this, but he sounds like an honorable guy." He pursed his mouth. "I hope I don't regret these words, but I feel like you should go see him."

"Why do I have to be the one to go see him? He's the one who acted all weird after the kiss."

"It sounds like you acted weird, kicking him out the next morning and taking offense to being called tall."

Sage winced. She stood and went in the house. Her bungalow was barely bigger than her cabin—living room, small kitchen, three bedrooms cramped in the back, and a bath. It had also been her grandparents. The other grandchildren took the money her grandparents had diligently saved throughout their lives. Everyone agreed to let Sage have the small house and cabin. It was a dream come true for her. She loved these pieces of her grandparents much more than a pile of money.

"So, you'll go see him?" Levi asked.

"I'll think about it."

They continued talking, but Sage's mind kept straying to Cam. Did she dare go see him? What if he didn't want to see her and things became even more awkward between them? She almost wanted to savor the memories of what might have been rather than seeing him and knowing for certain that they could never become what she yearned for.

CHAPTER TWELVE

Cam was grumpy. He'd had a glimpse of what it could be like to be with a smart, fun, and beautiful woman, and for some unfathomable reason, he'd messed it all up. Luckily, his shifts Tuesday and Wednesday were busy and kept his mind a little bit distracted.

His sister had called him half a dozen times, but he'd been on calls every time and hadn't been able to answer. Then he decided he really didn't want to talk because she always pulled crap out of him, so he put off calling her back.

By Friday night he couldn't stand it anymore. He knew she was going to be ticked if he interrupted her out on a date with one of her numerous wannabe boyfriends, but he couldn't stand stewing about Sage one more minute. Caylee would drag it out of him and give him advice. He pressed her name on his phone and paced his front yard. He loved his yard. It was a natural landscape with tons of trees and no manicured grass. He simply mowed the weeds and planted more wildflowers. Actually, it was a bit out of control, the only thing in his life that wasn't structured and by the rulebook.

Caylee answered on the third ring. "You don't answer my calls for a week. Then you call when I'm at the Cheesecake Factory? You're interrupting Linda's Fudge Cake."

Cam laughed. His beautiful, feisty sister cracked him up. Her wild, curly, dark brown hair, with streaks of red and gold, matched her personality perfectly. "I thought I'd better call you back. Who are you with?"

"His name is James. He's okay. A little too high on himself and his financial portfolio. The food's fabulous though, so I can handle a bit of pompousness. What's up?"

"I can't just call because I'm missing my sister?"

"Ha! Like you ever do anything random or spontaneous."

Cam thought about kissing Sage. Caylee would be proud of him for that instinctive moment.

"What's her name?"

"Excuse me?"

"You wouldn't interrupt my date if you weren't really in deep. You found someone you like?" Her voice pitched up in excitement.

"I hardly know her," Cam said, though he felt like he knew Sage better than he knew most of his crew. "But she's fun and smart and beautiful."

"Then what's wrong? Why are you calling me instead of taking her on a date?"

"Well ... I kissed her."

Caylee squealed. "You teasing me?"

"No, I really did kiss her."

"Wait. Was it after the appropriate number of dates, running a background check, and asking her father's permission?"

"Nope." She'd been teasing him about not being spontaneous his entire life. He didn't mind proving her wrong with Sage. "Haven't been on an official date. Haven't met her dad. For all I know she's an embezzler."

Caylee laughed. "Yes! Good job! Oh, yeah, that's my boy."

Cam smiled, imagining her doing a celebration dance.

"And what happened after you kissed her?"

"Then I insulted her, I think. She seems to be sensitive about her height. I don't know." He pushed a hand through his short hair. "I suck at this stuff, Cay."

"I know you do, big man. But if you like her half as much as your voice says you do, maybe you should call her and take her out tonight. Beg her forgiveness for being a dumb oaf and definitely kiss her again."

The roar of an engine brought his head up. A red Jeep pulled into his driveway. Cam's eyes widened, and then he smiled. "Good news, Cay. I've got to go."

"What?"

"She's here."

"Oh, yeah, I like it. Go, Cam! Go, Cam!"

He hung up amidst her cheers. The Jeep pulled to a stop, and the door swung open. Sage's long legs encased in skinny jeans were the first things out—they kept coming and coming. Cam was completely enjoying the show. Seconds later, Sage strode toward him, clutching his sweatshirt. Cam couldn't believe how much he'd missed seeing her beautiful face. His eyes swept over her high cheekbones, pink lips, and deep brown eyes. She didn't meet his eyes, but shoved the sweatshirt into his hands. "You forgot this."

Cam held onto her hand with the sweatshirt between them. "Thank you."

She finally focused on him. They were silent as she seemed to question him with her glance, and he hoped he reassured her. He wanted to be with her, and if he'd offended her, he was sorry. Did he really have to say the words? He thought of Caylee cussing him and pushed out a breath. "Okay."

"Okay?" Sage questioned. She had the most expressive eyebrows, dark brown and arched in what he thought was a perfect way. Right now, those eyebrows were drawn down close to her eyes.

"I'm sorry," he said very repentantly. *That should do it, right?*

"Sorry for?"

Oh, man. She wasn't going to make this easy on him. Cam set the sweatshirt on the porch and took both of her hands in his. Her eyes widened, but luckily, she didn't go all girl on him and ask a million questions. "I offended you somehow, and I honestly don't know what I said wrong."

Sage's beautiful smile burst onto her face. "My brother said I was too touchy about it."

"About what?"

"My height." She glanced down.

Cam froze. Was she just giving him a hard time? This perfect specimen didn't know she was perfect? "Your *height*?" He really didn't know how to respond. He wasn't the flowery kind of guy. Not at all.

She pulled her hands free. "Never mind. It's stupid. I should go." But she didn't move to walk away.

Cam touched her arm, sweat breaking out on his forehead. This was important, and it seemed like it was up to him to make her understand. Him. He'd never said the right thing to a woman, but Caylee was screaming in his head now, so he gave it a valiant effort.

"Sage. I'll probably say this all wrong. I'm not the charming, complimentary kind of dude." He paused, but she still didn't look at him. He took a deep breath and plunged ahead. "You are the most beautiful woman I've ever seen, and your height is perfect to me. I love you being tall, and your shape is amazing."

Sage was definitely looking at him now. "I think you said that pretty well actually."

Cam exhaled. "That's a relief." They stood there for a few seconds, her smiling and him wondering if he could kiss her again, but Caylee would tell him it was too soon. What was the next logical step? How did he keep her close so sometime soon he could try for another kiss? "Can I take you to dinner?"

She nodded slowly. "Sure."

Cam was the one grinning now. He'd done it. He'd said the right thing, and she'd agreed to go out with him. "Do you have any place you'd like to go?"

She tilted her head, and her eyes filled with a challenge. "I've heard Pineapple's has great food."

Cam swallowed. Ah, no. He wouldn't mind showing her off to the other firefighters, but Pineapple's wasn't what he had in mind for a romantic date. "You don't want to go to Pineapple's."

"Why not?" She folded her arms across her chest. "I thought it was where all the firefighters ate."

"Yeah, to hang out with the guys, but you wouldn't like it. They'd all, um, stare at you."

"So *you* like that I'm tall, but now you're going to try to protect me from other men staring because I'm, what did your buddy Porky call me, Gigantor?"

"Whoa. Okay." Apparently he hadn't set her straight earlier. Dangit. Why couldn't he make her understand? Why did women need constant reassurance? "You need to listen to me, and you need to listen hard."

She blinked at him and tilted her head to the side. "I'm listening."

There was a challenge in her voice, and once again, he knew he had to say this right. His hands were clammy as he started. "You are the most gorgeous, perfect woman I have ever seen in my life. When men stare at you, it's not because you're too tall, it's because you are so beautiful they want to stare until they've imprinted your face in their memory for life." Hey, for a non-emotional captain he'd done okay. He was warming up to this compliment stuff.

Sage blinked at him again, but this time it was because moisture was rolling out of her eyes and down her silken cheeks.

Cam touched that soft cheek. "Hey, don't cry."

Sage threw herself at him. Cam caught her and half-laughed, loving her lean body close to his. "Okay. I guess you actually listened to me this time."

Sage squeezed him around the neck then released him much too quick. "Thank you, Cam. My brother tells me all the time how pretty I am, but, well, you know, he has to say stuff like that because he's my brother."

Cam tried to remember the last time he'd complimented his sister or anyone. He needed to do a better job. Though he knew Caylee heard how beautiful she was from all the men she dated, and he doubted she was lacking in the self-confidence department.

"Come on, Coach Captain." Sage nudged him with her shoulder. "I'm driving."

First she dragged two huge compliments out of him, the likes of which he'd never imagined, and his fellow firefighters would fall over if they ever heard, and now she was driving? Emily always drove the fire truck, but when he went on a date, he drove. It was just the way it was.

"Okay," he said, walking to her door and swinging it open.

Sage gave him a flirtatious, half-confident and half-shy smile that yanked him in harder than he thought was possible. Maybe he'd never been on a third date with someone. Maybe he'd never had a woman drive him on a date. Maybe he'd never handed out gushy compliments. Today they were all streaks he was more than happy to shatter. The guys at the fire station bought each other ice cream for anything that was a first. He kept thinking someone owed him a lot of ice cream right now. Probably Caylee. He grinned as he climbed into Sage's Jeep.

CHAPTER THIRTEEN

Sage floored it out of Cam's driveway, fishtailing and laughing as he scrambled for his seatbelt. She was glowing from his compliments. She didn't care if any other man in the world thought she was too tall, Cam obviously didn't, and it felt amazing to hear, especially since he wasn't the type of guy to shout out empty flattery. That bit about men wanting to imprint her face in their memory? Wow. Maybe *O, Captain, My Captain* would've been an appropriate response.

The cool wind rushed through the open Jeep as they pulled onto the highway and headed toward Pineapple's. She really wanted to go there with him. Wanted to see him amongst his co-workers and feel the atmosphere of the place. Levi used to go there when he came home to visit before he was deployed. He'd always wanted to be a firefighter, but was recruited to the Air Force Academy on a football scholarship and had used the military to get through medical school and residency. After that, he had stayed in the military life for the past eight years.

"I should've kept my sweatshirt," Cam said.

Sage slowed down a little bit. "It can get cold in here."

"I like that you drive a Jeep."

Sage glanced at him. He looked good in her Jeep, filling up the passenger seat. His deep blue eyes sparkled at her. She was falling for this guy much too fast, but who could blame her with the sweet lines he'd just said and how great he was in the different capacities she'd seen him in.

"Got to indulge in my wild side." She winked.

He chuckled. His cheek crinkled irresistibly. "I was pretty sure you had one. So tomorrow I'm taking you on an adventurous date."

"You're getting a little ahead of yourself. Let's see how tonight goes before we make any promises for tomorrow, Coach Captain Compton."

He laughed again.

Sage felt carefree, happy, and just all-around good. *Thank you Levi for pushing me to go see Cam.* She pulled into the parking lot of Pineapple's and noted that it was filled with a lot of trucks, Jeeps, and sport utilities. "Where are the mini-vans and Cadillacs?"

Cam jumped down and hurried around the Jeep to help her out. "You'd get razzed for years if you drove one of those."

He took her hand, and they walked toward the front door. Sage couldn't believe the difference between the almost crushing feeling she'd had earlier tonight, wondering if she'd ever go out with Cam again, to right now feeling like he was her boyfriend or something. He smiled broadly at her as he opened the door, and Sage felt like he was taller somehow than the six-four she'd given him credit for when they first met.

She glanced around at all the firefighter t-shirts and paraphernalia on the walls. The delicious scent of grilled meat wafted over her. "Yum, it smells good in here."

"Pineapple is a fabulous cook. I keep trying to get him traded to my crew. Everybody fights over him."

"I bet." She inhaled deeply again.

A cute blonde welcomed them, and they followed her to a table in the back.

A yell rang out. "Woo-hoo, Cap! You got a date with the hot Gigantor?"

Sage's body stilled and went hot and cold in the worst possible way.

Cam squeezed her hand. "Excuse me." He nodded to the blonde. "Jamie, will you please seat my date and get her a drink?"

"Yes, sir." Jamie nodded to him.

Sage followed Jamie and sat. She saw Cam grab Porky by the arm and pull him around the corner to a back room. Cam's deep voice carried to where she was sitting, unfortunately in the closest booth to the back room. She wondered if the rest of the restaurant could hear.

"You'll treat my girl with respect, or I'll smear your face across the parking lot. Got it?"

"Sorry, Cap. I didn't mean anything by it. I mean, come on, she is tall."

"Never call someone a derogatory name, JFK. Especially a woman. It hurts them."

"Got it. Sorry, Cap. She is hot though. Good job landing her."

"*Don't*, JFK."

"Okay, yeah."

Sage busied herself looking at the menu as JFK sauntered past her booth, pausing to give her an obnoxious wink like he hadn't just been reamed. Cam appeared a few seconds later. He sat and gave her a forced smile. "Pineapple's burgers are amazing."

"Not feeling the red meat draw today. How about the grilled chicken skewers?"

"Really good."

She nodded then couldn't help herself. "'My girl?'"

Cam's face went a little red. "Sorry. I was trying to get a point across."

"I don't mind."

Cam's dark blue eyes focused completely on her. "Yeah?"

"Yeah." She nodded, and they were lost in their own silent conversation when Jamie returned to take their order.

The rest of dinner went great. Emily, Jake, Tyler, and some other firefighters came over and introduced themselves. Cam was fun to talk to, sharing some hilarious firefighter stories with her then laughing loudly at her stories of Levi teaching her how to make dry ice bombs and him getting in trouble when she blew up their parent's mailbox.

They both were a lot more relaxed throughout the meal than they had been in all their previous interactions.

After dinner, she drove him back to his house and parked her Jeep. She really wanted to kiss him again, but how did she get in a position for that? Walk him to the door? Lean over the gear shift? Every idea seemed awkward.

"Your house is beautiful," she said.

"Thanks. I did all of the framing and finish work."

"Nice." He was handy. Another item to add to the list of impressive Cam qualities.

"So, tomorrow afternoon about one? The big, adventurous date?" He grinned.

Sage tilted her head to the side. "I'll be ready."

"See that you are, and no backing out this time." He commanded.

"Aye-aye, Cap."

He laughed then swung his door open and climbed out.

"Thanks for dinner," she said.

"I owe you at least one more for feeding me last weekend."

"Sounds good." They stayed there smiling at each other for a few seconds. When it started to get awkward, he slapped his hand on the Jeep then stepped back. Sage took that as her cue to leave. She slipped it into reverse and flipped around. As she drove out of his driveway, she glanced back. He was standing there watching her go. She could really see herself liking this guy.

CHAPTER FOURTEEN

C am rapped on Sage's door and waited. He'd coached a game down in the Salt Lake Valley this morning, but the entire afternoon, evening, and hopefully into the night was planned for Sage. She swung open the door, wearing those fitted running clothes that got his blood pumping and a large smile. Her blonde hair was up in a ponytail, but its shiny length spilled over her shoulder.

Cam reached up and touched her hair. It felt as smooth as he'd imagined it would. "You do realize when you dress like this I can't concentrate?" Cam couldn't believe those words had leaked out.

"What do you need to concentrate on Coach Captain Compton?" She winked at him. "Your lacrosse game is over, and you aren't on call today."

"Good point." He didn't want to get all cheesy and clarify that all he wanted to concentrate on was her.

He walked her to his truck, opened her door, and helped her inside. They drove up the mountain to Olympic Park.

"This is your adventurous date?"

Cam smiled. "I know it's not true adventure if you're safe, but the buddy I usually get climbing gear from had already rented it all out today. I'm hoping we can go on a hike from your cabin tomorrow after-

noon, I'm sure you'd love to take me Jeeping, but I don't think I'm
brave enough to sit shotgun for you."

"Oh, I think you're plenty brave." She winked. "So we're spending
tomorrow together too?"

"Getting a little ahead of yourself, Miss Turner. Let's see how
today goes."

Sage laughed at him using her line as he grinned broadly at her.

Cam paid for their adventure tickets, and they started with a ride
up the ski lift for the alpine slide. They caught an occasional glimpse
through the pine trees of the metal slide and the little sleds that
raced down.

"Ladies first," Cam gestured with his hands when they disembarked
from the lift and walked to the top of the slide.

"No way. You go first and see if I can catch you."

Cam scoffed. "You can't catch me. I'm double your weight. You're
not *that* good of a driver."

"Let's see," she said with a mischievous grin.

Cam looked at the young male attendant who was eyeing Sage like
she was Miss America. "Good luck, man. My money's on her."

Cam climbed onto the little sled with a handle that was his brake.
He suddenly worried if he was too big for this contraption. He didn't
have any time to stew about it as he took off, gaining speed quickly and
wheeling around the corners. He had to pull on the brake a few times
or he would've flown off the track. He was a few turns from the
bottom when he heard a loud whoop and whipped around to see Sage
bearing down on him. Her hair floated behind her and her face was lit
up. Cam was a goner on the challenge, but in even worse danger of
losing his heart completely.

She rammed into him as they pulled into the stop. The attendant
scowled at them, but didn't say anything. Sage laughed and laughed.

They went to the zip line next and just hearing her light laughter as
they swooped down the mountainside was pure joy to Cam. The lush
green valley spread below them. He didn't know that he'd ever felt this
way. Being with Sage made him happy and then some. He felt more
alive than when he dragged a hose line into a burning building, never
completely sure if it would be the last time he saw daylight or not.

They plunged off the drop tower, and Cam cracked up when Sage screamed the entire way down. She even conned him into climbing around the adventure ropes course with a bunch of eight-year olds, laughing at him when Cam got stuck between some ropes because he was too big.

It was so carefree and fun. Cam loved every second of it.

"Okay, last thing," he said. "Can you handle the tubes?"

She glanced up the green mountainside. It looked like a turf lacrosse field, even though it was definitely some other kind of material. She grinned. "Where do I sign up for that?"

"This way."

They climbed into a four-wheel drive utility vehicle, and their guide, Kayden, joked with them as they drove to the top. They got situated together on a huge tube, and before Cam knew it, they were off. Sage was laughing, but Cam was gripping the tube and half-terrified as they plunged down the mountainside. They reached the bottom, and he felt a little disoriented, like he was floating or something. He stood and grabbed her around the waist, pulling her close. "You are crazy."

"Crazy fun."

"Yes, that too." He'd never had so much crazy fun.

Cam leaned down, fully intent on kissing her.

"Hey, friends." Kayden yelled as he pulled to a stop next to them and jumped out of the side by side. "Did you love it?"

"It was exhilarating," Sage said.

Cam wondered if he was imagining how breathless her voice sounded and the implication of her words. Was he exhilarating to her? Oh, how he hoped. Tonight, he was taking her to dinner, and she had better plan on being kissed good and long when he took her home. He grinned to himself.

CHAPTER FIFTEEN

Sage opened her door and about had a heart attack. "Wow. You look ... wow."

Cam grinned, and it didn't help her pulse slow down at all. He was wearing a suit so deep blue it was almost black. It matched his eyes and looked like it was tailor made to showcase his large, fit body.

"Look at you." He took her hand and squeezed it. "You're so beautiful."

Sage smiled and did a little curtsy. Her knee-length red shift dress floated up. She was wearing heels. Heels! She'd never dared wear them, but Cam claimed he loved her height, and he was tall enough she could wear a two-inch stiletto, and he still had her by several inches. "I dress to please."

"I'm definitely pleased." He chuckled and escorted her onto the porch. She teetered a little bit on the stairs.

"Sorry. Not used to wearing these shoes."

"You should always wear them. Your legs are ..." He looked away and cleared his throat. "Perfect."

"Thank you." Sage smiled, wishing she dared tell him it was only because of his confidence boost that she'd been brave enough to don the funky black and white swirled stilettos.

He helped her into his truck, and they drove down to the Redstone shopping area by the outlet stores. "Do you like Italian?" he asked.

"It's a personal favorite."

"My sister loves Ghidotti's, so we come here every time she's in town."

"I've never been."

"Good." He gave her a quick glance and a warm smile. "I like introducing you to new things."

Something about that smile and those words had her tingling.

The young man running the valet service got her door and helped her out. He handed her off to Cam with a smile that grew when Cam palmed him a twenty-dollar bill.

"Whoa. You tip the valet that much?" Sage asked as the young man jumped into Cam's truck.

Cam shrugged, looking embarrassed. Sage reddened too. "Sorry."

"No, it's okay. I like rewarding young people who are willing to work, but I don't want you to think I show off my money."

Sage's eyebrows dipped. What was he talking about? She hoped firefighters made a fabulous wage for the expertise they had and risks they took, but she doubted they were super wealthy. They probably didn't make much more than she did working as a public servant. Cam's truck and house were both really nice, but she assumed that was because he was single and could sink all his money into them. Plus, he'd said he had done some of the work on the house.

The maître d' escorted them to a corner table. The restaurant was gorgeous with decorative wrought iron along the banisters and over each archway, tan-colored walls, marble pillars, a huge fireplace, and green plants decorating the surfaces.

The Italian waiter was fun and flirtatious. Sage had to hide a smile when Cam scowled at the man complimenting Sage and beaming when she said she'd have whatever he suggested. He returned quickly with their drinks and a calamari fritti appetizer.

Sage dipped some calamari in the sauce and savored the creamy texture and spicy flavors.

"Can I ask you a question?"

"Sure." Cam focused in on her, and she thought how incredibly lucky she was at this moment to be with this hard-working, kind, and handsome man. She hoped her question didn't mess anything up, but he'd already dropped a couple hundred dollars at the Olympic Park without batting an eye.

"Do you have a side job I don't know about?"

He shifted in his seat and glanced down. "No."

"I hope I don't make this awkward, but your comment about not trying to show off your money. I didn't know firefighter captains were ... wealthy?"

Cam shook his head. "You're right. The pay is fine, some complain about it, but it's fine. I, um." He cleared his throat. "When my parents were killed, I got a lot of insurance money, and the money from their estate and investments was substantial."

Sage's eyes widened, and her heart seemed to falter. "Your parents were killed?"

He nodded shortly and took a quick drink of his Italian soda.

"I'm so sorry." Sage managed. She felt like she knew Cam, but obviously she didn't.

"It was a long time ago," he said dismissively.

Sage could tell he was trying to act like he was okay, but he obviously wasn't. She didn't know if it was the time or place to try to open him up.

The waiter brought her shrimp ravioli and his chicken parmigiana. Cam started telling her about the lacrosse game from this morning and how Braden knocked some kid down with his stick then did a warrior yell. He got a penalty, but Cam couldn't help laughing about it.

The mood lightened, and they enjoyed talking about her students, his sister, her brother, and her parents throughout the meal, but she still wanted to know what had happened to his parents.

The night went too quickly, and before she knew it, they were on her porch.

"I hate to say goodnight. I could sit and stare at you in your suit for hours."

Cam's grin was her favorite. His cheeks crinkled, and his eyes seemed to sparkle at her. He gently ran his hands down her arms. "Maybe we should dress up for dinner every night."

"You're saying we're going to be eating dinner together every night?" She took a bold step closer.

"I'm game." He lowered his head, and his warm breath brushed her cheek.

"Cam?" she whispered, encircling her arms around his neck.

"Yeah?" His low voice rumbled over her.

"I'm falling for you pretty hard."

Cam studied her with an intensity that left her breathless. "Don't worry. I can catch you."

He pressed his lips to hers, and the world exploded in light and color. Tucking her against him, he took the kiss from unreal to the stuff of poetry as he caressed her lips with his own. Luckily, he was holding her against him or she would've fallen over on the unfamiliar heels. It didn't matter if everyone else in the world thought she was too tall or too big, she was the right size for Cam. With how strong and capable he was, she knew he could catch her no matter how hard she fell for him.

CHAPTER SIXTEEN

Cam went to church with Sage and her parents the next day. He liked her dad and felt instant sympathy for the big, tough guy who couldn't move very well anymore. Her mom was fun—average height, thin, and very capable. Cam could see where Sage got her beauty and her sparkling personality. He'd hoped to have dinner with her alone at her cabin Sunday afternoon, cook for her and prove that food could still be good when following a recipe, but her mom insisted they have dinner with them at their house. Although he'd have liked to get her alone, he didn't mind too much. It was nice to be part of a family like this.

"I don't know why you think you have to drive," Sage complained as he got her door. Taking her hand, they sauntered together up her parent's sidewalk. She looked as fabulous as she had last night. Today she was wearing a knee-length pencil skirt and a pink blousy thing.

"I the man. I must drive." Cam grunted out.

Sage patted his hand. "I hate to tell you, dear, but it's the twenty-first century. The cave man act isn't as sexy as it was in the nineteen-fifties."

"Shoot." Cam grinned at her. "Sorry, I just like to drive."

"Me too, and my Jeep is a lot more fun."

"I freeze in that thing."

"You are such a wimp." Sage winked and then poked a finger at him and laughed teasingly.

Cam whipped her off her feet, holding her against his chest.

"Put me down." She commanded.

"Not until you admit that I'm a tough guy." He really just wanted to hold her in his arms, loving that they were at a spot where he could tease and hold her without feeling awkward.

Sage shook her head resolutely, her eyes full of laughter. "Scrawny wimp who can't handle a little cold."

Cam let go of her upper body with his right arm. Her head swooped down, and she let out a squeal. Cam caught her and lifted her back up and into his chest. "I'll really drop you this time." He warned.

Her cheeks were pink, and she was laughing. "You wouldn't dare."

He threw her up into the air then caught her a little bit lower. "Say that I'm tough."

She wrapped her arms tight around his neck and shook her head stubbornly. Cam didn't know that he'd ever been this carefree and happy with anyone. "Say I'm tough, or I'm going to ..." He couldn't think what to threaten besides dropping her, and he really didn't want to let her go. "Kiss you on the face."

"On the face?" She chuckled. "Oh, the threats."

"Say it." He commanded, pulling her up and in tighter.

Sage brushed her nose against his cheek. "No way, I'm waiting for you to kiss me on the face. Never had that happen before."

Cam smiled, anticipation surging through him. "You've got to the count of five to say I'm the toughest man you've ever met, or I'll kiss you in ways you've never been kissed."

"Ooh. Lucky, lucky me." She winked.

"5, 4, 3, 2, 1." Cam counted fast and hoped her parents weren't anywhere close to the front door as he lowered his head and kissed her until she let out the cutest moan and they were both short of breath. Feeling a little unsteady from the heady sensation of kissing and holding her, Cam set her on her feet, trailed his hands through her silky hair, and kept right on kissing her.

"Church in the morning, making out by afternoon." The teasing voice came from behind Cam.

Cam and Sage broke guiltily apart.

Her dad was leaning against the doorjamb, smiling. "Your mother says you need to come eat and stop smooching or the rolls are going to be cold and the butter won't melt properly."

Sage rolled her eyes and took Cam's hand. "First she demands we eat dinner here. Then she ruins a good kiss."

Her dad chuckled and turned, walking slowly back into the house.

Cam tugged Sage to a stop. She glanced up at him with those dark brown eyes, and he knew he was a goner.

"Only a *good* kiss?" he asked.

Sage's beautiful face broke into a smile. "Forgive me. Kissing on the face was amazing."

Cam kissed her lightly again. He wanted to get lost in her, but her dad cleared his throat from the entryway, and he realized he'd better focus on impressing the parents before he continued showing their daughter how much he liked her.

Sage thought that dinner with her parents went really well. She was glowing from Cam lifting her and throwing her around like she weighed nothing and the amazing "kissing on the face." Her parents noticed how happy she was, even if they were shocked that she'd brought a man to church and Sunday dinner since she'd never done either. Cam and her dad fell into easy banter about the Broncos and the 49ers. Cam had apparently been a Broncos fan even before they were good, but her dad still had to raz him. Her dad thought every-body who liked the Broncos was a bandwagoner.

She liked watching Cam interact with her mom and dad. Even in her parent's house, he had that aura of being in charge, but he was very respectful to her dad no matter how much her dad teased him, and he complimented her mom on her cooking and her beautiful yard.

It was interesting, though, how good he was at avoiding much talk about himself. Even her mom, who could've dragged a confession out of a nun, couldn't get him to open up about his past. He'd give a short answer then change the subject. It killed her. Was he embarrassed, uncomfortable, or just an ultra-private person? She wanted to know everything about him, but how to pry without making him lock up even tighter?

After they helped clean up dinner, they went on a lazy Sunday walk along the historic rail trail. Cam took her hand, and Sage smiled. Things were comfortable, yet exciting with him. If their relationship kept progressing like this, maybe she wouldn't wait for Levi to get home and give his approval of Cam.

"What are you thinking?" Cam asked, nodding to a man with his Saint Bernard on a leash.

"I like being with you Coach Captain Compton."

Cam grinned. "Good, because I plan on spending a lot more time with you."

"Do you now?" She tilted her head to the side and studied him. "What if I say no?"

"Nobody tells the Captain no."

She laughed. "What would happen to somebody who told you no?"

Cam shrugged. "I don't know. It's never happened. I guess I'd make it a direct order."

Sage shook her head. Cam tugged her to a stop. The trail was quiet, and they were shaded by birch and pine trees. He gazed down at her with a warm intensity that had her quivering with anticipation.

"If I asked to kiss you, you wouldn't say no, would you?" His voice had dropped low and husky.

"I'd have to think about it. What would my punishment be if I dared to say no to 'O Captain, My Captain'?" She couldn't believe she'd just said the line she'd been thinking so often when she was around him.

Cam smiled and traced his hand along her neck and into her hair. Her neck tingled. "I'll make you polish the bumpers on all the trucks at the station."

"That doesn't sound fun." Sage took a step closer, only inches separated them, and she had to lean back her head to keep focusing on his eyes. "But I don't work for you, so you have to think of something else."

"I'll tell your students about their crazy teacher who drives like a bat out of Hades and breaks the law parking in front of fire hydrants." He cupped the back of her head with his palm and aligned their lips. She could feel his warm breath on her mouth.

"You wouldn't. That's just low, mister."

"Don't tell me no, then."

Sage smiled. "Hmm, if I must give permission—Coach Captain Cameron Christian Compton, I hereby give you permission to kiss me." She lowered her voice. "Any time you want."

Cam was so close his lips brushed hers when he smiled. "Thank you, Miss Turner."

He kissed her so thoroughly neither of them heard the bikers until they almost ran into them. "Coming through!" The lead guy yelled.

Cam lifted Sage off her feet and whirled her behind him. The bikers dodged past them. Sage's heart was beating fast, but almost being run over by the bikes had little to do with that. She loved the sensation of being swept off her feet and protected by her firefighting stud.

"You just instinctively take care of people, don't you?"

Cam turned to her. His eyes trailed over her face. "I will always take care of you, Sage."

She bit at her lip. "You can catch me?"

"Definitely."

Then he was kissing her again, and she didn't care who came on the trail. She was going to enjoy each second.

CHAPTER SEVENTEEN

Monday morning Sage was floating on a cloud. To say spending last weekend with Cam was the most incredible of her life was a massive understatement. She tried to focus, but her class seemed to sense that she was off her game, and they were wired. The spring fever didn't help. Even though they had a month of school left, they were all ready to be playing outside, not cooped up in a classroom.

Braden was especially crazy. Teasing with everybody, and she honestly thought he was physically unable to sit still. Sage loved the kid, so she didn't want to punish him, but she had to keep him under control or she'd lose control of the entire class.

"Braden!" She forced her voice to be stern, even though she was hiding a smile. He'd been imitating the principal, and though Principal Jensen was a fabulous guy, his voice was high-pitched and his eyebrows were constantly drawn together. Braden's imitation was spot on.

Braden glanced fearfully at her. Though he loved to tease, he did not love to be reprimanded. He seemed to crumple. "I'm sorry, Miss Turner."

"If it happens again, you won't participate in class store on Friday."

His lip trembled as he nodded somberly and then focused back on his math sheet.

Sage's insides took a hit. She hated threatening, especially Braden with the class store. His mom made beautiful bracelets and necklaces, and the girls would run up the bidding on them every week, leaving Braden with lots of class money to buy treats, toys, or whatever else was for sale. For a kid who struggled financially in an extremely affluent area, class store was heaven. His one opportunity to blow money, albeit fake money, on anything he wanted.

Twenty minutes later, she sent the class to art and heaved a sigh of relief. She loved her students, but sometimes a teacher needed a break to recoup and figure out how to teach her students something when she understood how much they'd rather be out in the beautiful spring air. She was right there with them.

Sage closed her eyes for a few seconds and simply pictured Cam's face. His dark blue eyes were sparkling at her and those lips, oh, yum. He'd made her promise to come to dinner at the fire station tonight. She didn't look forward to seeing that JFK guy, but she wanted to get to know Cam's crew. They were like his family in a lot of ways. Frowning, she wondered when he was going to tell her more about his parents. At least, he'd shared a lot about his sister.

The fire alarm shattered her moment of quiet. Sage jumped to her feet. Nobody had told her about a drill today. She pushed out of her door and ran toward the art room. It was through the circular foyer and almost on the opposite end of the school from her classroom.

The smell of smoke reached her before she saw the cloud, hovering like a misty demon in the hallway where her children were supposed to be. She sprinted toward the smoke, but someone grabbed her as she dashed through the foyer area of the school.

Sage tried to pull free. "My students!" Looking down at the arms around her waist, she realized whoever was holding her was in fire-fighter gear. She peered over her shoulder through the face mask. It was JFK.

He said something, but she couldn't understand him through the mask. He picked her up and tried to carry her out of the building, but he obviously wasn't as strong as Cam and couldn't move her very effectively.

Sage hit him. "No! My students are in there." Her voice was clogging up with emotion. How bad was the fire? Were her kiddos in danger? She'd reprimanded Braden. What if that was the last thing he heard her say?

JFK dragged her outside, shoved her against Eli, one of the male teachers, and gestured at him to hold her then turned and ran back into the building.

"Sage?" Eli questioned. "You okay?"

"My students are in the art room."

Eli's eyes widened.

"Is that where the fire is?" She demanded.

"That's what I heard." He nodded.

"No!" Sage screamed out, trying to break free, but Eli effectively restrained her. She could see flames and smoke billowing out of the window that she was certain was the art room. Many of the children were lined up outside, some crying, some staring in shock. None of them looked injured, but amidst the chaos none of them were lined up with their class like they were supposed to be.

"I'm sure your class got out." Eli reassured her, but Sage didn't believe him.

More firefighters spilled out of the building, several of them carrying children from her class. She ripped her arm from Eli's grip and ran to them. "Janie!"

The little girl glanced up at her. "Miss Turner." She sobbed.

"Are you okay?"

She nodded, tears tracing down her soot-streaked face.

The firefighter sat her on the grass, where EMTs were gathering around the children who were burned and checking for severity.

"Is anyone else in there?" Sage asked the little girl.

She nodded again. "Stuff exploded, and Mrs. James got caught under the desk. She yelled at us to run, but Braden wouldn't leave her. The fire got really bad."

More firefighters came out carrying children. Sage recognized Cam even with his gear on since she'd seen him wearing it before. He set Yvette on the ground. Sage ran to him, grabbing his arm. He turned and glanced down at her.

"Braden!" she said loudly so he could hear her over the noise.

He glanced around the yard and said something she couldn't understand.

"He's not here. Janie said Mrs. James was trapped under a desk, and Braden was trying to help her."

Cam nodded and took off at a run back into the school, looking like a human tank with all of his gear on.

Confusion reigned around her. Sage tried to reassure the students gathering around her, but she continually watched the front door for some sign of Cam and Braden. After several excruciating minutes, she couldn't wait one more second. What had gone wrong? Where were they?

"I need you all to go sit by the flagpole," she instructed. "And I'll be right back."

They obeyed quietly, obviously subdued by the scare. Glancing around to make certain Eli or JFK wouldn't stop her, she crept toward the building. Then when she was sure she wouldn't be stopped, she ran through the foyer and down the hallway toward the art room. The smoke choked her. She coughed and had to slow her steps, but she couldn't give up. She had to help Cam find Braden. Isabella couldn't survive without Braden, and Sage couldn't survive without Cam.

———

Cam hustled back into the classroom. He thought everyone was out, but if Sage said Braden and the teacher were still in here, he had to look. The smoke was so thick he couldn't see anything. He dropped to the ground and started searching, yelling into his mic. "Powers! JFK! I think there are still people in here. Get back in and help me search."

"Got it." JFK responded immediately.

"Almost to you," Powers said.

Cam army-crawled around the room, seeing little jean clad legs in the corner. He scurried to the body. Braden. His shirt had caught fire. No! Cam beat the flames out then dragged him free of the debris and picked him up. He was completely non-responsive. Cam had no clue how bad the burns were, but he couldn't stop and let worry overtake him right now.

He ran in a crouch to the door with the little boy and collided with Powers. The smoke was so thick they hadn't seen each other until they were on top of each other. Handing him off, he said, "Take him. I think the teacher is trapped."

JFK appeared. "Let's go, Cap."

Cam turned to lead the way. They had to drop to hands and knees for visibility to cross the last twenty feet. Sure enough the teacher's body was trapped under a desk. The metal was so hot, Cam was certain his gloves were going to melt. He strained against the desk. It didn't budge. JFK turned and pushed with his back. The desk groaned and shifted.

"Do that again!" Cam shouted.

With an audible grunt, JFK put everything he had into it. Cam pushed with his hands and the desk cleared just enough for Cam to grab the woman's leg and drag her free. She was badly burned. He had no clue if she was alive or dead. The desk fell back with a crash, and Cam lifted the woman's torso and wrapped her up from behind like he was about to do the Heimlich. JFK grabbed her legs and they shuffled through the smoke and out into the hallway where there wasn't much better visibility. For the hallway to get so much worse in the little time he'd been in the room, conditions were deteriorating quickly. The building would probably be a total loss. If the battalion chief hadn't already gone defensive and pulled out all of the attack crews, Cam was going to recommend it. Halfway down the hallway, he stumbled over something, but righted himself and kept going.

"She's not a lightweight," JFK muttered.

Cam didn't respond. He conjured up a quick prayer that the woman and Braden both survived.

They finally cleared the building and the EMTs met them with a stretcher. Cam didn't have time to look and see if the woman was going to be okay. He pulled off his helmet and mask as he hurried to the principal. "Did your teachers do a head count? Is everyone accounted for?"

"Yes. Braden and Mrs. James were the last."

Cam pushed out a breath. The adrenaline leaked out and he had

time to process it. Braden! Was he okay? He hurried toward the ambulance, looking around for Sage.

"Sir!" A male teacher approached him. "One of the female teachers
went back in there."

Cam looked around desperately for Sage.

"Miss Turner," the guy said, confirming his fears.

Cam rushed toward the building. Sage! What was she thinking?
"Powers! Emily! Old Guy! JFK! Sage is still in there!" While in motion,
he slid his face mask back on then got his helmet in place.

He could see his crew rushing in after him and heard their
responses but didn't register them. Sage. He couldn't lose her. All the
memories of that night rushed back. The firefighters carrying him and
Caylee out. His parents' bodies finally being brought out. Burned.
Smoke inhalation. Echo condition. He couldn't remember all the
words the firefighters and EMTs had flung around that night, but it
had all equated to no hope for his family.

Not Sage!

Please, Lord. He prayed. *Please help me find her.*

He suddenly remembered stumbling over something in the hallway.
As he thought about it, it could've been a body. Pressurized smoke shot
past Cam as he made entry, and even through his turnout gear, he
could feel the heat. The thermal layer was dropping and fast. If anyone
was still alive in there without fire gear on, they wouldn't be for long.

Dropping to the ground, he searched below the smoke layer, which
only gave about eighteen inches of clear air. Sage lay sprawled on the
industrial carpet. The flames were nowhere near her, but he knew as
well as anybody that smoke inhalation could be deadly.

He reached her body and picked her up in his arms, hurrying back
toward the entrance. "I've got her," he said into his mic. "Clear out."

His crew responded, but all Cam could focus on was Sage. Two
ambulances were screaming away from the scene as he carried her
body outside.

"No!" Cam yelled, desperate to help her. "She needs to be transported immediately. Get me some oxygen!"

"We've got more ambulances coming." Emily's voice was soothing, but it didn't help. She keyed her mic to let command know they had brought out another victim.

Cam set Sage gently on the grass, knelt down, and ripped his helmet off. He had to focus, but the fear was overwhelming, and darkness edged into his vision. Despite the heat of the fire and the sweat soaking everything he was wearing, his body was cold. He pulled off his gloves and felt for a pulse. It was there.

"Cap?" Jake, a paramedic from B Platoon tugged at him. "Let me look at her."

"No!" Cam elbowed him away. He leaned down and put his cheek against her nose. The sweetest breath he'd ever felt brushed against his cheek. "She's got a pulse, and she's breathing," he told Jake.

"Okay. That's good, Quad C. The ambulance is two minutes out. Let's get some oxygen started on her. It'll be okay, Cap."

It wasn't okay, though. She wasn't awake. Was it the smoke, or did she have another injury? Cam's hopes and dreams were fading and imploding the longer she lay there unresponsive.

Cam forced himself to scoot out of the way. Jake grabbed the oxygen, placed a non-rebreather mask at fifteen liters per minute over her face, and Cam found himself holding his breath as oxygen filtered into her lungs.

The high-pitched squeal of an ambulance cut through the smoky air.

"Miss Turner?" A little girl's voice cried out. Soon other children were joining in the cry, some wailing and sobbing for their teacher.

Cam lifted her into his arms and hurried to meet the ambulance. Jake followed, holding the oxygen tank. They rolled to a stop, and Jake was opening the back door for him. Cam hefted her up and onto the gurney and started looking for a pulse oximeter.

"Cap. Let me help her," Jake said. "I know where everything is."

Cam recognized he was right, but he didn't want to turn Sage's care over to anyone. No matter how competent they were.

The EMTs from station four were at the back of the ambulance.

"Let's go!" Cam yelled at them. "She needs a hyperbaric chamber."

"Okay." The guy climbed in with them and the girl, Cam thought her name was Heather, slammed the door, and within seconds, they were driving off.

Jake checked her pulse and put a blood pressure cuff on then glanced up at him. "You know her?"

Cam nodded, glancing down at Sage's beautiful face. She looked okay, just pale and unresponsive. He really needed her to wake up. He couldn't take this stress much longer. "What are her O$_2$ stats?" he asked.

"Eighty-three percent."

Cam blew out a breath and uttered another prayer. Anything below ninety percent was a bad sign, and with all the carbon monoxide in fire gasses, her true oxygen saturation could be much lower. What if they didn't get to the hospital and a hyperbaric chamber soon enough so they could push the carbon monoxide out? He'd fallen for her much too fast. What if he had to survive without her? He'd always been a believer and knew that his parents were in a better place and all that kind of junk, but it was excruciating to be the one left behind. He couldn't let Sage go. It was just unacceptable to think of living without her.

The ambulance weaved as they flew down Parley's Canyon. Cam grabbed for a hand hold as one vicious turn threw him.

Sage coughed shallowly, and Cam pushed closer to her. "Sage?"

Her body was suddenly racked with coughs. Cam's hopes spiked. Her coughing fit looked miserable, but it was actually a very good sign.

"That's it, baby, clear those lungs."

Jake glanced sharply at him, but Cam didn't care. *Please help her*, he repeated over and over again in his head, a desperate prayer to a God he'd never given up on, no matter how low things had gotten for him.

Cam pushed an arm underneath the gurney to keep her stable and elevate her upper body as the ambulance continued to weave down the canyon. The coughing continued for several minutes. Cam winced as her body was racked with the coughs, but he was grateful she was coughing.

"Up to eighty-eight," Jake said.

Cam nodded. He'd take any improvement. Sage's coughing

subsided, and she blinked, opening those beautiful brown eyes and staring up at him. "Cam?" she whispered.

He squeezed her hand. "I'm here." His shoulders sagged, and he felt almost weak with relief. She was awake. "You're going to be okay."

She gave him a wan smile, and her eyes fluttered closed. Cam held her up as coughs continued to expand her chest. Her eyes flew back open. "Braden?"

"I got him and the teacher out. They'll get to the hospital before us, and we'll find out how he's doing."

"Okay."

"One minute out." Heather called back to them.

Jake readied her oxygen for transport as the ambulance rolled up in front of the emergency room entrance. The doors popped open, and Cam had to release her as they lowered the gurney out and the three paramedics rolled her through the doors.

"Cam," he heard her whisper.

Cam started forward. He needed to be with her. Jake stopped him with a hand on his chest. "Wait here for just a minute, Cap. I'll come get you."

Cam's eyes widened. Yes, Jake was the medic and had more expertise in this situation, but Cam was used to giving the commands.

"She'll be okay. There are plenty of us." Jake gave a dry chuckle. There were always too many people standing by to help when they got to the emergency room. "But maybe you need a minute?" Jake's green eyes said he understood somehow. "Give us just a few minutes."

Cam didn't answer. He stopped in his tracks and watched her disappear through the double doors. She was going to be okay, and Jake was right. He needed a minute, or maybe much more than a minute.

He sank onto a chair. His body started trembling. He'd almost lost her. He tried to push the memories away. He couldn't think about his parents right now. His stomach tightened like somebody had gut-punched him. He couldn't do this. He'd let himself fall for Sage, and she'd almost died in a fire. All of his nightmares came back to assault him, and his shoulders bowed with the anguish of it.

His body started shaking like a recovering addict going through

DTs. He had to clench his fists and flex his muscles to stop the trembling. Sage. He couldn't lose her. It wasn't possible to survive another loss like his parents. He said a prayer of gratitude that she was okay, but he didn't believe he could handle loving and losing again.

CHAPTER EIGHTEEN

Sage watched her oxygen levels rise as the hospital staff poked, prodded, and did about a hundred tests on her. There had to be twenty different people in and out of her room for the first few minutes. It didn't take long for the crowd to die down, and with her oxygen levels rising, they didn't end up putting her in the chamber they had been talking about.

"Where's Cam?" she asked the fireman with the bright green eyes who'd stayed with her. Her throat hurt, and her voice came out all scratchy, but besides that and being really tired, she felt okay.

"He's in the waiting room. You can see him soon."

"Can you go get him?"

"Sure." He nodded and disappeared. A few minutes later he returned. Sage searched behind him for Cam. The green-eyed guy shrugged. "I'm sure he's close by. He was really concerned. He'll come find you."

The curtain was swept aside, and Sage's heart lifted. He was here. But instead of her broad-shouldered firefighter, a round-faced nurse bustled in. Disappointment tasted bitter as the nurse checked her blood pressure for the fiftieth time and kept claiming that she was doing great. She'd be doing great when Cam came.

Cam never appeared. Sage was released an hour later with instructions to rest and drink lots of fluids. She was grateful she was alive, but she wanted Cam with her.

Her parents showed up. Thankfully, they brought some clothes for her as the hospital had cut hers off and given her an awful sweat suit she could wear home. She changed into her own clothes, then signed a bunch of papers, promising the hospital personnel that she had insurance and she would send them the information as soon as she got her purse.

Her mom fussed over her, and her dad tried to act tough, but he kept giving her arm a squeeze. "Your young man around here?" he asked.

"I thought he was." Sage didn't have her phone, so she couldn't text or call Cam. She remembered waking and seeing him in the ambulance with her, his eyes filled with concern and anguish. But as soon as she got into the emergency room, he was gone. Where had he disappeared to?

"Are you okay to wait while I go find out if Braden and Mrs. James are all right?" she asked. A little break from her mom's anxious glances would be nice, and she really needed to check on her student and fellow teacher.

"Sure thing," her dad said, settling himself into a couch in the emergency room waiting area. "We'll catch us up on some People Magazine reading."

Sage smiled. "I'll come find you right here then."

"Sounds good."

Her mom gave her one more hug then let her go. Sage went to the information desk and then slowly walked to the elevator and the Burn Center. An older nurse with long, gray hair braided down her back escorted her to Braden's room.

"He's doing really well for the amount of burns he received," the nurse said in response to her queries.

"What about the teacher who was brought in with him?"

The nurse shook her head. "She's alive, but ..." She left it at that, and Sage's stomach turned. She didn't know Mrs. James very well, but she was a nice lady who'd been doing art for years. She had a large family that she liked to share pictures and stories about.

"The little guy's on a lot of painkillers, so he'll probably be in and out of consciousness, but he's going to come out of this with only a few scars."

"Thank you. That's wonderful to hear." Sage pushed through the door and saw Braden stretched out in the bed. His monitors were beeping slowly. Cam sat in the chair next to the bed, his head bowed and his wide shoulders rounded like the weight of the world was capable of bowing even his strength. He was still in his firefighter pants, but his coat was sitting on the floor beside him.

"Cam!" Sage exclaimed, so excited to see him that she yelled too loud for the quiet hospital atmosphere.

His head jerked up and then he was on his feet, gathering her into his arms. "Sage." He breathed out, kind of choking on her name. "You're okay?"

Sage clung to him. "Yes. Thanks to you, I hear."

Cam pulled back and searched her face. He gave her a grim smile, and then he was kissing her, and there wasn't room for any pain, sorrow, or worry when he was doing that.

"Coach?" A little croak broke them apart.

Cam yanked away from Sage and hurried back to Braden's side. "Hey, buddy."

"Hi," Braden whispered. He smiled groggily up at her. "Miss Turner."

"Hi, sweetheart." Sage came over and touched his arm, wondering where his burns were and how extensive they were. "Are you doing okay?"

"Hurts." He managed.

"I'm sorry, bud." Sage rubbed his arm. "You were so brave trying to help Mrs. James."

"I tried, but the desk was too heavy. Is she ... okay?"

"Yes." Sage lied.

Cam glanced up at her. She shook her head. Braden didn't need to deal with any other worries right now. They'd have to pray Mrs. James recovered so Sage wouldn't receive a black mark on her heavenly record for lying to an innocent child.

When she glanced back at Braden, he was asleep again.

"He's been in and out?" she asked.

"Yeah."

"Is Isabella here?"

"She's been here the entire time. I told her I'd sit with him while she went to the restroom." Cam kept his focus on Braden. Sage self-ishly wanted him to concentrate on her.

"That was nice of you," she said slowly.

Things were suddenly stiff between them. What was going on? Cam had disappeared earlier when she really wanted him to be there for her, and now, he wouldn't even meet her gaze. Why was he so excited to see her a few minutes ago? Why had he held her and kissed her and now seemed like he didn't even want her around?

Isabella pushed into the room from behind them. "Miss Turner? Oh, I'm so glad you're okay." She gave Sage a brief hug.

"I'm fine. I just got minor smoke inhalation. They told me one breath of hot air is enough to knock a person completely out."

"Why did you go back in?" Cam's voice was stern, and she felt like she was one of his crew members who'd disobeyed an order. He chose that moment to finally look at her, but it wasn't warm or welcoming.

"The nurse said Braden is doing well." Sage directed her comment to Isabella, ignoring Cam's question because she really didn't have a good answer besides that she was scared, confused, and couldn't not try to help.

"Yes. He's going to be okay. Some bad burns on his abdomen and back where his clothes caught fire, but thank heavens Coach Compton went back in him for him." She gazed up at Cam worshipfully.

Cam stood and cleared his throat. "I'm going to walk Sage out."

"Okay."

"Do you need anything?" Sage asked.

"No. The nurses and Coach are taking good care of us. Thank you."

"I'll check in with you tonight," Sage said.

"Thanks again." Isabella sank into the chair Cam had been sitting in, reaching out and holding her son's hand.

Sage was so grateful Braden was okay. His mom was a sweetheart, and Sage sure loved that boy.

Cam didn't touch her as they walked out of the burn unit and down a short hallway. She really could've used that touch, some reassurance that things were still good between them.

"I'm going to stay here with Braden and Isabella tonight," he said, not looking at her.

"I'm sure they'll appreciate that. Do you need a ride back?"

"No. Powers and JFK brought my truck down."

"Okay." She clenched her hands together, wanting to reach out to him, but feeling extremely awkward for some reason. Where had her Cam from this past weekend gone?

"Do you have a ride home?" His gaze brushed over her then returned to the wall behind her.

"Yes, my parents are here."

"Good. Okay, then."

He turned to walk away. What on earth? Sage grabbed his arm, not willing to leave things like this between them. "Cam?"

He glanced back. "Yeah?"

"Um, what ... what happened?"

"What happened?" His brows drew together.

"You're acting really remote." That was a nice way of putting it. He was acting like he wanted nothing to do with her. Like they were strangers and this stilted conversation was all they had between them. If Cam was pulling away from her, it would kill her surer than the smoke.

Cam drew in a breath then slowly let it out. "I ..." He shook his head. The silence stretched until it was more than awkward, and then he flung out there. "Why did you go back in the school, Sage?"

Sage drew back. What did that have to do with their relationship and why he was suddenly so cold? "I had to find Braden."

He stared at her with narrowed, cold eyes. "That was my job. You didn't have protective gear, training, an air tank." He shook his head and then kind of hung it like somebody had beat the happiness out of him. "You know, I thought you were great because you're brave and like taking risks, but I can't be with somebody like that." He blew out a breath. "I can't lose someone I love again."

"What are you talking about? I'm not some crazy person who throws myself into danger." She had done that, but only because she'd been so consumed with worry about him and Braden and ... Wait a minute! He'd said he loved her, but yet he couldn't be with her?

Cam studied the wall again. "I can't do it, Sage. I'm sorry." He turned and walked away from her.

Sage was confused, and then she was ticked. She rushed after him, catching him just before the Burn Unit door. "You can't do *what* exactly?"

"I can't have a relationship with you, Sage. It's not worth it."

Sage drew back like he'd hit her.

Cam's face softened for a fraction of a second. He reached his hand up and brushed her cheek. "I'm sorry." Then his jaw hardened, and he turned and marched through the hospital doors.

Sage sat there in shock. Fat tears rolled down her cheeks as she wondered what had just happened between her and Cam, and why she wasn't worth it.

CHAPTER NINETEEN

Cam went through the next few days on autopilot. The chief sent someone in to cover the rest of his shift, and he stayed with Braden and Isabella at the hospital. He went home at night to sleep and shower. The little guy recovered amazingly fast. He would have some scarring on his abdomen and back, which was something Cam could relate to. The good news was the emotional scarring from the fire should be minimal, especially when they got the news that Mrs. James was out of intensive care and was going to recover. The older teacher would have a lot of skin grafts and would probably not return to school, but she'd survive. It was more than could be said of Cam's parents. What he wouldn't have given to not feel the survival guilt. Thank heavens Braden wouldn't experience that.

By Thursday afternoon, Cam was able to drive Braden and Isabella home and get them settled in their little apartment. He went to the grocery store and stocked the fridge and pantry, hiding five one-hundred dollar bills underneath one of Braden's schoolbooks where they should find it. He made sure that the hospital knew that anything not covered by insurance was to be sent to Cam for payment. Hopefully Isabella would be okay without her normal income over the next week.

He thought about Sage twenty times an hour. No. That was an under-exaggeration. She never left his thoughts. He ached for her. He wanted more than anything to go to her and tell her the pain and agony of loving and knowing you might have your heart ripped out might be worth it if he could be with her, but he wasn't brave enough. Was it really worth it? He'd lost his parents. He couldn't handle losing someone else he loved. Loving Caylee like he did was enough of a risk, but he couldn't break up with his sister.

His phone rang as he pulled into his driveway Thursday night. He pushed the button on his wheel, and Bluetooth picked it up inside his cab.

"Hey, sis."

"How are you? I heard about a huge fire at the school."

"Yeah. It was bad. One of my players got burned. I just got him and his mom home from the hospital."

"That sucks."

He looked out his window at the forest around his house. Caylee had no idea how bad this entire situation sucked.

"But he's okay?"

"He'll have some scars, but he's doing pretty good."

"Then why do you sound so down?"

Anger flared inside of him. "Not all of us brush off fire and burns as easily as you do."

"Whoa. Just because I deal with my emotional crap better than you doesn't mean I brush off Mom and Dad's deaths."

Cam sucked in a quick breath. He picked up his phone and pushed a button so the Bluetooth disconnected and then swung his legs out of his truck and hopped down. He and Caylee didn't go here very often, and he needed to be on the move if they were getting into deep issues. He hated deep issues.

"You there?" she asked, her voice small and suddenly very childlike. Cam was transported back twenty years ago to after the accident when they were living with Grams and he'd find Caylee crying in the night. He'd hold her until she fell back to sleep.

"I'm here," he said quietly.

"This fire bringing back stuff you don't want to deal with?" she asked.

"Sage was in it." He admitted, striding up and down his yard. When he reached the forest, he'd spin on his heel and cruise the other way.

"Ah, no." Caylee was quiet for a little while then asked, "But she's okay?"

"Yeah, but ... her and I." He shook his head even though she couldn't see. "We're not okay."

"What did you do?"

"I told her it wasn't worth it."

Cam expected wailing and gnashing of teeth. The quiet on the line was worse. Finally, Caylee said, "Oh, Cam. Do you know how cruel that is?"

"I didn't do it to hurt her."

"Yes, you did. You did it to protect yourself."

She was right, and he knew it. He'd hurt Sage to keep himself from feeling more pain. He was a jerk. But being without her was much more painful than he could've imagined, even when he'd been in that ambulance freaking out about her dying. Had he made a mistake telling her love wasn't worth it? Even if he didn't want to fall in love, he was already there. He'd passed the point of no return and now being without Sage was an ache that was far worse than his fears.

"How do you deal with relationships so well?" he asked his sister.

Caylee gave a short bark of a laugh. Completely unladylike and much too real. "I never let them go past the fun."

"That's why you date so much?" It made a lot of sense.

"You got me. It's sadly true. I burn through them, and if they try to get serious, dump them quick."

"Oh, sis, you're not much better off than me." They were a pathetic pair. But how else did someone deal with life besides shutting down and avoiding future pain?

"Worse, I'd say." Caylee had some life back in her voice. "You found the right woman for you. I don't think I'll ever find a man worth getting serious."

"I really do hope you find that man someday." He paused then questioned quietly. "But how do you know she's the right one for me?"

As he said it, he knew. He'd found something with Sage that was worth it. She made him laugh and not have to follow every rule, and he'd fallen in love with her. She was worth it, no matter what it cost him. He needed to tell her that and quickly.

"I know, all right? Sister's intuition." He could almost sense Caylee rolling her eyes.

"What should I do?" He'd hurt Sage. That thought ripped through him, but all he could do was move forward and try to repair the damage.

"What all men should do—beg your stinking guts out. And chocolate, flowers, and diamonds never hurt."

Cam laughed. It felt unfamiliar but really nice. The laughter spilled out, and Caylee joined him. When the laughter had burned itself out, Cam said, "I love you, sis."

"I love you too. Go get her."

Cam hung up the phone and smiled. He would. Now he just needed to pray that she'd forgive him.

CHAPTER TWENTY

Sage came home from the hospital dejected and depressed. Her throat healed quickly, and after a few days of being lazy, she was ready to get back into life. It was obvious Cam felt something for her, but for whatever reason, she wasn't worth struggling past his doubts or worries. Luckily, Levi didn't call because he probably would go AWOL to come and kick Cam's rear. That image actually made her smile.

School was closed until they could figure out where to hold it as they replaced the wing of the school that had burned to the ground. With her house clean and her parent's house clean and their yard looking impeccable, she didn't know what else to do but go to her cabin. She deep-cleaned the cabin, cooked and baked up a storm and took long hikes. It was gorgeous outside, and even the occasional spring rain storm didn't stop her exploring the trails.

Sometimes out in nature, she'd forget about Cam for a few seconds, but then it would return with the force of a jackhammer. Man, she loved him, and he'd turned into a big old jerk. He was a good guy—saving others, being a coach, and taking care of Braden and his mom, but to her overly sensitive heart, he was a dipwad. Unfortunately, thinking of every dumb name she could call him didn't help her feel better at all.

Slowly making her way back to her cabin, she decided she'd bake banana bread. There was already way more food than she could ever eat, but cooking or baking helped a little bit.

As she pushed through the last grove of pine trees, her jaw dropped wide. A huge silver Chevy truck was parked next to her Jeep. Her eyes searched quickly around the yard and cabin, and finally she found him sitting on her porch swing.

No. He had no right to be here. Not after telling her she wasn't worth it. He had no right to make her hope that they might have something between them.

She forced herself to keep walking toward him when all she wanted to do was turn turkey and run back up the trail. She steeled her spine. It was better to deal with him then get back to her wallowing.

Their eyes met and held. His dark blue gaze was as intriguing as ever. He slowly stood, and Sage took it all in. The way his quadriceps muscles flexed as he straightened, his large, well-built chest and shoulders looking like they wanted to cradle her, his handsome face so familiar yet so exciting to her. She wanted to hate him, but she didn't know if she had it in her.

Sage stopped ten feet away from the cabin. Cam walked slowly down the stairs. Then he was there, within touching distance. Would she ever have the right to touch him again? No, that was wussy girl thinking. He didn't have the right to touch her after saying she wasn't worth it. *He* wasn't worth it. The good-looking piece of dog meat.

"Sage." There was so much loaded into the way he said her name— he missed her, he wanted to talk to her, but he was scared and uncertain.

Sage should've softened then. The look in his eyes was certainly soft and welcoming, but it ticked her off. She'd been wallowing, crying, and miserable for days. He'd broken her, dumped her, and he thought he could come back here and say her name all squishy and she'd rush into his arms? Bull stinking crud!

"What do you want?" She spit out.

"You."

Sage drew a ragged breath. He was good. She'd give him that. She tossed her hair like an angry bull and took a step closer to him. His eyes widened, and his appealing smile crossed his face. She wasn't falling for it though. Then she made the mistake of inhaling—the musky, manly scent about did her in, but she was tougher than that. She kept rowdy children in control all day long. She could stay strong against one buff firefighter.

"You can't have me," she said, her voice deceptively calm.

Cam's smile slipped. He swallowed and reached out his hand. Sage dodged his touch, backing away. If he touched her, she might falter. She wasn't faltering. She wasn't falling for him again and then letting him tell her she wasn't worth it.

"Why?" she asked, unable to control the angry words. "Why did you build me up, tell me I was pretty and you liked me being tall, pretending that you liked me, and making me fall so hard for you, just to smack me down like that?" She didn't tell him everything. That she'd never been as happy as she'd been with him. That she loved him so desperately she didn't know if she'd survive without him.

"I ..." Cam shook his head. "It wasn't you. It was me."

"Ha!" Sage burst out. "You think you can make things better with that lame line? It's not you. It's me. You're dang right it's you! You're so wrapped up in your tough firefighter mountain man image, you think you can just make me fall for you then ditch me when things get tough."

Cam nodded. "You're right, and I'm sorry."

"Dang straight I'm right, and you should be sorry!"

Cam smiled again. "Does that mean you'll forgive me?"

She gasped, incredulous. "No! I'm not forgiving you. I'm not falling for your tricks again. Just because you're some hot firefighter you think you can draw any woman in and then dump her? Well, I've got a news-flash for you. I'm not one of your little groupies." She wanted to break down and cry, tell him how much she'd missed him and how she would forgive him if he'd just smile at her like that, but she wasn't going to allow herself to be drawn back in.

"Sage." His voice was tender again, and she had to fight with every-thing in her to not go gooey. "I don't draw women in and dump them. It's only you. You're the only one for me."

The words were right, but she wasn't ready to buy them. Not in the least. "You're a liar."

"Excuse me?" His brow furrowed, and she could tell she was starting to tick him off. Well, good, she was tired of being the only one frustrated, confused, and irrational in this conversation.

"I'm not the one for you." She shot at him. "You can't even confide in me what happened to your parents. If you want a relationship, you need to talk to that person about everything."

His mouth thinned, but he said nothing.

Sage stepped forward, grabbed his shirt, and yanked it up, revealing the scars on his otherwise perfect abdomen. "You can't even tell me how you got these. Occupational hazard? I'm not slow, Cam. You wear those protective suits. You wouldn't get burned on your stomach."

Cam kept staring at her. She released his t-shirt and stepped back, knowing that she'd gone too far. His burns were something so sensitive, he couldn't tell her about them. She hurt for him, but she needed someone who could trust and confide in her. "If you wanted me, you should've given me all of you. You can rescue other people, but you're never going to let someone rescue you."

His eyes darkened, but he still didn't answer.

Sage was embarrassed, mad, and regretting half of the angry words she'd just hurled at him, but she couldn't stand here one more second or she'd probably throw some more. She whirled from him and ran back up the trail she'd just walked down. She was already out of breath from all the emotions. She was gulping for oxygen within a minute. Her lungs were definitely not healed.

Cam's loud footfalls came behind her. Sage increased her pace, but it wasn't enough. Cam caught her, grabbed her around the waist, and whirled her around to face him.

"You want to know about my scars?"

Sage pulled in a quick breath. "Not like this. With me forcing it out of you. I'm sorry. It's too late, Cam."

"It can't be." He held on to her waist and kept her facing him. "It can't be, Sage. I love you."

Sage shook her head. He loved her? More lies. Yet she couldn't find it in her to pull away from his warm grip.

"My parents were killed when I was eight." He released her and clenched his fists. "Our house caught on fire in the middle of the night. The wiring." He drew in a ragged breath and pushed it out. "I don't know what woke me, but I saw the smoke, and I remembered what the firemen had taught our school class. I dropped down to the ground and crawled to Caylee's room. I pulled her off her bed and dragged her toward the hallway. She woke up, and we were trying to get to my parents' room when everything seemed to explode. I guess my dad was still conscious and had opened their door. The fire had started in their room. The fire whooshed out and my shirt caught. Those flames took my dad. I don't know when my mom died. Caylee has scars on her hands from trying to beat the flames out on my shirt. The firefighters came in then and rescued us, but it was too late for my mom and dad." He lifted his shirt up and showed her the scars again then dropped it back down and almost glared at her. "I've never shared that story with anyone."

Sage hadn't moved during his story. She wanted to go to him and comfort him, but she didn't know if he'd welcome her touch after she'd told him off pretty harshly a few minutes earlier. "I'm so sorry about your parents."

His wide shoulders lifted and lowered as he pulled a long breath in and out. "Thanks."

They stood there staring at each other. Time seemed to stretch and pull, thick like taffy. Sage closed her eyes and then took a step forward. She opened her eyes and drew in a breath, needing more bravery than when she'd tried to rush into a smoke-filled building to save Braden and Cam. "You like to rescue people. Can you rescue my heart? It got fried a few days ago by a hot firefighter."

Cam's handsome face cracked into a small smile. "My training on rescuing hearts is sadly lacking."

Sage nodded. "I've noticed. But I think I can help. It's a practical course and very hands on."

"Really?" One of his eyebrows lifted, and his smile grew. "Mouth to mouth resuscitation involved?"

"Oh, definitely." Sage bit at her lip and wanted more than anything to fling herself into his arms.

Cam opened those very appealing arms wide. Sage uttered a little gasp, and she wasn't sure if she'd moved or he had, but she was encircled in his arms, pressed against his chest, and his lips found hers like they'd practiced this every day for a year. But there was nothing practiced about this kiss. It was needy, hungry, yet tender and full of light and promise. Sage stood on her tiptoes to bring him closer, loving that she needed to make herself taller.

Yapping dogs registered in Sage's mind from somewhere far away yet too close. She and Cam jerked apart as her nearest neighbor's Great Dane and Alaskan Husky went yelping past them like the hounds of Hades were on their heels.

"What in the world?" Sage gave a shaky laugh and pushed some hair out of her face that had come loose from her ponytail in the heated exchange with Cam.

Cam laughed too, but then his eyes widened as he focused on something behind her. "Sage!" He yelled, grabbing her hand and tugging her down the trail. "Run!"

Sage obeyed, keeping up with his sprint. She had no clue what she was running from and imagined everything from a bear to wolves to rabid dogs. The sound of thundering hooves was growing louder. Sage glanced over her shoulder and saw a moose charging at them. Its head was bowed and it was coming fast. Sage had no clue how they were going to outrun it.

Because she wasn't watching where she was going, her foot struck a boulder, and she lost her balance and went down hard. Cam was still holding on to her hand and tried to pull her back up, but the moose was on them. Cam dove on top of her and curled his body around her. Sage was insulated from the brunt of the attack, but could still feel the moose kicking and stomping on them. Sage screamed out then bit at her lip and held on to Cam's arms.

Cam went slack on top of her, and it was all she could do to not start screaming again. The attack seemed to have stopped, but she didn't dare move. She wondered if she could move with Cam lying on top of her like he was. She listened hard and heard the moose stomp away.

Sage was more terrified now than she had been during the attack.

Why wasn't Cam moving? She pushed and squirmed out from under him.

"Cam?" she whispered.

He was on his side, his eyes closed. His clothes were torn, and his body looked battered like he'd just been thumped in an awful fight, cuts and scrapes all over, but mostly on his face. Had the moose hit his head or was he unconscious from his other injuries? No, oh, no. He'd been trying to protect her.

The only first aid training she had was from some continuing education course she'd taken, but she knew she needed to check for a pulse. Had she and Cam really been joking about mouth to mouth resuscitation minutes before?

"Oh, Cam, wake up." She begged. Pushing her fingers against his neck, she was at least reassured with a strong pulse. Leaning down, she put her cheek against his nose and sighed with relief again. He was alive and breathing.

She glanced around. Her cell phone was back at the cabin, but her neighbor's cabin was closer, just through the trees. She hated to leave Cam, but she couldn't move him on her own. Standing quickly before she could second-guess it, she ran for the cabin and prayed that Cam would be okay and that horrible moose wouldn't come back.

Her neighbor was out in the yard with his dogs. "Dang fool things," he said in way of greeting. "I think they musta come between a moose and her calf or something. They came yipping into the yard like a bear was gonna maul them. I've been tracking that moose and her baby just up the hill from us. You don't want to mess with them, you hear?"

"Mr. Keller, call 911! My boyfriend got mauled by the moose."

"You kidding me right now?"

"No! Call them, please. He's just up the trail." Sage turned and ran back toward Cam, praying her neighbor would listen and Cam would survive. He might have internal injuries, brain trauma, who knew? As she knelt by his side and prayed harder, she grew even more understanding of how hard it was on him when she'd been the one injured and unresponsive. But no matter how scary it was, being with him was worth it. If the Lord would only let her be with him again.

CHAPTER TWENTY-ONE

Cam fought his way out of a dense fog. He could hear voices but they were far away and distorted. One of those voices had to be Sage's. He focused on it. She was calling to him. He could swear he could smell her, that unique sweet pear scent. He'd never noticed many smells with his sense of smell damaged, but he'd been close enough to her to notice and memorize her smell.

He kept fighting and finally he pushed his heavy lids open and, through gritty eyes, peered out at the white-washed room. Hospital. He should've guessed. His body ached like he'd been run over by a freight train, especially his head. It throbbed with every heartbeat.

He tilted his head and searched for Sage. She wasn't there, but Caylee was smiling at him, blinking back tears. Caylee crying? That hadn't happened since she hit fourteen.

"You're awake."

"Yep." He groaned.

"They said when the drugs wore off you'd come around, but oh, Cam, I was so scared." Caylee laid her head down on his chest and sobbed.

Cam lifted his heavy arms and wrapped them around her. "Hey, it's okay, sis. I'm okay."

She yanked back up and half-smiled, half-glared at him. "Don't you ever do that to me again! What would I do without you? How would I survive?"

Cam cracked a smile. It hurt. "You do realize I'm in a pretty dangerous profession." Talking hurt too, but he was okay. He could sense it was just bruising, nothing broken. He must've been unconscious when the helicopter crew picked him up, and they probably sedated him then let him slowly wake up. He'd ask for details later, but the important thing, now that he was awake, was that he see Sage.

"Yes! And I pray my guts out morning, noon, and night for you."

"I didn't know you prayed."

She shook her head and offered him a drink of water. Cam sucked down the cool goodness. It was heavenly. Thinking of heavenly. "Where's Sage?"

"She ditched you because she couldn't handle the emotional burden of seeing someone she loved being hurt."

"Seriously?" Cam's heart was thumping hard.

"No, you dork. She's not lame like you."

Cam smiled. He sure loved his sister.

The nurses came in and exclaimed over him waking up. They took his blood pressure and reassured him that his vitals were all normal then took out his catheter and got him up and to the bathroom. He really did feel okay and was happy when they agreed to remove his IV. He asked for some juice then asked for somebody to find Sage. They all tittered over that and finally left him alone with Caylee.

"Where is she?"

"Her parents called. Don't worry. She'll be right back. She's been here stressing over you since you tried to play hero yesterday."

Cam smiled.

"She's a doll. I can see her being my sister," Caylee said with a broad wink.

Cam's insides warmed. Caylee approved. Sage had been in his arms before the attack. Now if only he could show her how he felt. But first he had to get out of this bed again, brush his teeth, take a shower, and find some real clothes.

"I don't want to talk to her right now."

"What!" Caylee exploded.

"Not like this." He gestured to himself. "Get me some toiletries, sis, and help me get cleaned up."

"Dude, you just came out of a gnarly concussion. She's not going to care if your butt is hanging out of your hospital gown."

"I care. This is one of those things you have to do right."

Kaylee rolled her eyes, but pushed the nurse's button as Cam elevated his bed and concentrated on ignoring the pain in his head and swinging his feet to the ground. He'd get cleaned up somehow. Then he'd find Sage and show her exactly how much he cared.

Cam wrapped his hands around the scratchy blanket and pushed it off of him.

"So, you really care about this girl, huh?"

"I love her, and I want to tell her that somewhere more romantic than a hospital room."

Caylee beamed at him. "You love her?"

He nodded.

"Well, let's get you cleaned up. Then you just need to talk to her and try to contain all your flowery expressions of love." She winked, knowing anything Cam said would *not* be flowery.

"Okay." A rush of excitement alleviated some of his pain as he thought of seeing Sage. The nurses listened to Caylee's explanations of why he needed to get cleaned up, but the young one was adamant. "He needs to get cleared by the doc if he wants to check out."

"No, I don't." Cam growled at her. "I can leave against medical advice anytime I want. If you want me cleared, find the doc."

"Okay." She hustled out of the room as the other nurse helped Caylee get toiletries set up for him in the bathroom. The hospital had some clothes for him. They fit horribly. The T-shirt was too tight on his shoulders, and the sweats were riding up on his ankles, but he couldn't be picky right now.

It was humiliating that the nurse insisted on staying with him while she cleaned him up, but Caylee had promised to go find Sage and take her to the courtyard. The nurse said it was pretty with flowers and benches. Anywhere but a hospital room to be with Sage.

CHAPTER TWENTY-TWO

Sage backed away from Cam's hospital room door. Caylee's voice cussing Cam out followed her down the hallway. *I don't want to talk to her*. Those lines repeated over and over again in her mind. Why didn't he want to talk her? What had she done now? Her being injured before had flipped him out and made him turn from her. Had him being injured done the same? All she knew was she couldn't handle this emotional roller coaster.

Cam had risked his life to save her, but that was his job. His instinct was to save. She loved him, and not just because of how heroic or handsome he was. She truly loved him. She shook her head and hurried down the hospital hallway. If he didn't want to talk to her, there was nothing she could do to change his mind. Tears flowed freely as she hurried to escape.

Sage's parents had brought her car last night, so she could leave if she needed to, or to take Cam home after he awakened, like they all had been hoping and praying for. Now he was awake, but it was nothing like she'd been hoping for. She should just go find her car and get out of here, but she was hesitant to leave. She wanted to give Cam the benefit of the doubt, but she really didn't know if she could handle a relationship with someone who kept saying things that hurt her, whether it was intentional or not.

She was pacing the hallway instead of leaving like she'd planned when Caylee came running toward her.

"Sage! Come with me." She dragged her away from Cam's room.

"What? Where are we going?"

"Cam's awake, and he wants to talk to you."

"Shouldn't we go to his room then?"

"He wants to talk to you somewhere nicer." Caylee winked at her and continued dragging her down the hall and into an exterior area that was filled with trees, bushes, flowers, picnic tables, and benches. "Okay. We need to wait here for a little bit."

Sage wanted to ask Caylee about what Cam had said. If he wanted to see her here, why hadn't he wanted to see her in his room? She hated to act insecure, but it was eating at her.

Her phone rang. She glanced at the screen and smiled. "This is my brother," she said to Caylee.

She pushed yes to answer the FaceTime call and smiled at his handsome mug. "Hey, Levi," she said.

"Whoa, he's a hottie," Caylee said over her shoulder.

Sage smiled.

"Who is that?" Levi asked.

"Caylee. She's Cam's sister."

"Hi." Caylee gave him a little wave and a flirtatious smile.

"Hey." Levi grinned, lifting his eyebrows in a suggestive way that almost brought a smile to Sage's face. "Nice to meet you."

"You too."

"Is Cam okay?"

"Yes." Caylee answered for Sage. "He just woke up, and he wants to talk to Sage *alone*." She drawled out alone like Cam was going to either attack her or ask her to marry him.

"No, he doesn't. I heard him tell you that he doesn't want to see me."

"What?" Levi and Caylee both exploded.

"Why would he say that?" Levi asked.

"No, you misunderstood the context." Caylee defended Cam. "He didn't mean it like that."

"Obviously it sounded like that to Sage. This is the second, or no, third time he's made her feel bad." Levi's brow was drawn down. "That's it! You're staying away from him, and I'm coming there on the next plane to kick his butt."

Caylee grabbed the phone from Sage's hand. "It's a misunderstanding. You don't need to overreact like some roided-up Neanderthal."

"Overreact?" Levi huffed. "I don't overreact. I'm the calmest person I know!"

"Ooh, think pretty highly of yourself, do you?"

"No."

Sage stared at Caylee and her brother on her phone. They were screaming at each other, and she didn't know how to fix the situation.

"Of course you do. I've dated Air Force pilots before. You're better than all of us lowly civilian folk. Your *parents* must be so proud." Caylee's voice dripped with venom.

Sage had gotten to know Cam's sister over the past two days, and she really liked her. She had no clue she could be so fiery and defensive. Obviously she was defending Cam and the way she'd emphasized parents was pretty telling, but did she have to attack Levi?

"Who *are* you?" Levi asked. "Give me back to my sister."

"No! Not until you say you're sorry and apologize to my brother."

"Apologize to your brother? He needs to apologize to my sister! He's the one who keeps breaking her heart, who doesn't know how to treat her right. Your dad must've completely failed on training him how to respect a woman."

"We don't have a dad!" Caylee yelled.

"Sage?" The deep, husky whisper came from behind her.

She whirled around and just drank in the sight of him. Cam had bags under his eyes, bruises on his face and arms, but his deep blue gaze was solely focused on her like she was the only woman in the world. She liked the way his too-small t-shirt emphasized his muscular shoulders. Taking a cautious step toward him, she ignored the verbal match behind her.

"I can't believe you're out of bed," she said.

He took a few more halting steps her direction. "The doctor wasn't very happy about it."

"We should get you back to bed." She crossed to him and held out her hand.

Cam took her hand, squeezing it gently. Warmth traced up her fingers and seemed to wrap around her heart.

"No. Not until I talk to you for a little while."

"Why do you want to talk to me now?" She couldn't help the defensive tone that crept into her words. She felt awful that he'd gotten hurt so badly protecting her, but she didn't want to hear his excuses for why he'd said something so hurtful again.

His eyes widened. "Why wouldn't I?"

"I heard what you said." She bit her cheek. "You didn't want to talk to me earlier."

"I didn't want to see you while I was laid out in a hospital bed. I do have a little bit of pride."

"Too much pride I'd say."

Cam gave a soft laugh and tugged her toward him. "We need to get something straight, beautiful girl."

Sage couldn't hide the smile that his endearment brought to her face, even though she was a little upset that he'd laugh at her. "What's that?"

"If we're going to be together, you're going to have to get over these insecurities."

Sage stared at him. "I've been dealing with them all of my life."

Cam wrapped his arm around her waist. "Well, you're done with them."

Sage's breath shortened. "How do you figure?"

He moved even closer. He didn't smell like his usual cologne, but he smelled clean and his breath was minty. "I'm going to spend every day telling you how beautiful you are, how much I love you, and how special you are to me, and you're going to believe me."

"Oh, really? Says who?" Now she was really smiling. He loved her, and he planned to spend every day telling her?

"I'm the captain. You have to obey me."

Sage laughed. "So, Coach Captain Cameron Christian Compton. I'm going to have to spend every day obeying you?"

He grinned. "Yep."

"What's my first order?" She mockingly saluted him.

"I'm hurting pretty bad."

"Oh." Sage felt awful. "Let's get you back to bed."

"No." He shook his head. "I need some kisses to make it better."

"Oh? I think I can do that. Where?"

He held out his arm that had a large bruise on it. Sage gently kissed it. Cam smiled and turned his head where there were scrapes down his neck. She kissed him softly there. Cam let out a soft moan that made her stomach smolder. He pointed to his cheek, and she kissed it. Cam grinned and pointed to his lips.

Sage laughed. "I don't see any cuts or bruises there."

"Doesn't matter. I'm the captain, and when I give an order, you have to obey."

Sage's laughter deepened. "O Captain, My Captain," she said before she kissed him and savored the warmth of his lips and the feel of his large hands pulling her in.

"I can see this is going to be a very well-balanced relationship," Sage said. "You giving orders and me fulfilling them."

Cam smiled down at her. "I love you, Sage. You have my heart. I'm going to spend my life following your orders."

"Oh?" Her heart was thumping hard at his tender words. They weren't ones she ever thought she'd hear from the tough Captain. "I didn't know a Captain knew how to obey orders."

"If I can be with you, I'll learn."

Sage gave him a quick kiss. "How about we just work together and nobody orders anybody around?"

"Sounds good." He kissed her back. "Unless I need kisses to make it better. I might have to order you around then."

"We'll make an exception then."

"I might need some more kisses right now."

"How many?"

"Let's start with twenty and see how that goes."

Sage smiled and kissed him. She lost track of time and kisses as she savored being in his arms.

"You two done with all the love talk? I think we'd better get this tough guy laying down again." Caylee's amused voice came from behind them.

"I'm feeling miraculously better." Cam nuzzled Sage's neck with his lips and held her close. "You done yelling at Levi?"

"I hung up on him." Caylee held the phone out. "Family parties should be fun with that guy."

Sage pocketed her phone. "We'll have to teach you two how to kiss and make up."

"Don't plan on it with that thick-skulled punk."

Cam laughed. "I guess I'll have to call Levi back and make amends for my family."

"Man, you are turning into some kind of wimp," Caylee said.

Cam focused back on Sage. "Don't tell my crew, but for this woman, I'll be a wimp."

Caylee laughed at them as Cam kissed Sage again. He could never be a wimp, but she loved knowing that he would do anything for her.

ABOUT THE AUTHOR

Cami is a part-time author, part-time exercise consultant, part-time housekeeper, full-time wife, and overtime mother of four adorable boys. Sleep and relaxation are fond memories. She's never been happier.

Sign up for Cami's newsletter to receive a free ebook copy of *The Feisty One: A Billionaire Bride Pact Romance* and information about new releases, discounts, and promotions here.

www.camichecketts.com
cami@camichecketts.com

EXCERPT OF RELUCTANT RESCUE

If you enjoyed *Rescued by Love*, read on for an excerpt of *Reluctant Rescue*, Caylee and Levi's story.

Caylee slunk to the back of the group, everyone but her anxiously awaiting the glorious return of their brother and son, Captain Levi Turner, from the battlefields of Afghanistan. She didn't like the guy at all, and she wasn't related so she didn't have to pretend he was perfect. But she did recognize and appreciate that he was heroic and honorable for serving their country in the military. She wondered what horrors he'd seen overseas and how that had affected him. Maybe that was the reason he was such a judgmental, overbearing, hypocritical grump.

Okay, she was being a little judgmental herself and she'd promised her brother Cam, and his almost-fiancée, Sage Turner, that she'd play nice. She groaned. It would be much easier to be nice if she didn't have to be here to see everyone gush over Levi and paste a plastic smile on her face.

Cam had already proposed to Sage, and of course she'd said yes, but they couldn't make it official until he got her brother, Levi's, "permission". How old school and cocky was this guy? Cam had already gotten approval from Sage's dad. What right did this high and mighty Air

Force physician have to determine if Sage and Cam got married? They were perfect for each other and she'd never seen her brother this happy. If Captain Turner dared to mess that up, Caylee would personally take him down. Dang, she was getting ticked at him again and he wasn't even here to defend himself.

Think positive thoughts.

Sage turned and caught her eye. "Any minute now," she said, smiling brightly.

Cam's broad arm was slung around Sage. They were such a perfect couple. Both tall and gorgeous, but most importantly, good people who truly loved each other and loved the Lord. Thoughts of Captain Turner flared in her again and she swore with a vengeance she wouldn't let him disturb their happiness.

Caylee gave Sage a weak smile and pushed her highlighted curly hair out of her face. She wished she could miss all the fuss and having to see Captain Turner's gloating, handsome face when he came down the stairs at the Salt Lake City airport. She wished he wouldn't have chosen to fly home commercially because then maybe they wouldn't have let her in the military compound. It would have been so easy to break a law, steal a candy bar or pack of gum so she wasn't approved to enter. Being in prison might've been preferable to this magical moment.

Her positive thinking wasn't working. She would run to use the bathroom, take an extra long time washing her hands, and meet them all by the baggage terminal. Maybe their ecstatic joy would wear down by then. She glanced at Levi and Sage's parents. It'd be hard to find nicer and more committed parents. Why did a jerk like Levi get a mom and dad like that and she and her older brother Cam, had nobody?

"I need to run to the restroom," she mumbled to Sage.

"Okay. We'll be right here."

"Don't worry about me if he gets here soon." They'd had word that his plane landed ten minutes ago so he should be there any second. "I'll meet you by the baggage claim."

Sage gave her an understanding smile. Caylee appreciated that Sage loved her brother, but her future sister-in-law was also sensitive to the fact that Caylee hadn't fallen head over heels for Levi during their one shouting match where he kept accusing Cam of treating Sage poorly. The man had no basis for his prejudice against her brother and he ticked her off. Cam was the best guy Caylee knew. He'd taken care of her since she was six and Sage made him so happy.

Caylee scooted away from the group, and when she was certain they were all focused on Levi's imminent approach, she rushed past baggage claim to the women's restroom on the far north end of the airport. Not the most fragrant spot to hang out, but much better than facing the handsome mug of Levi Turner.

She was washing her hands when she heard a faint cheer from the small crowd. Smiling grimly at the mirror, she muttered, "Well, he's here. Figure out how to play nice, chickie."

Pulling her makeup bag out of her red leather purse, she applied some powder to her shiny nose and touched up her eyeliner and lipstick. The eyeliner made her dark blue eyes pop, but it frustrated her that she cared what she looked like. It would be much better to not give this man any kind of attention, but feeling confident was crucial when going into battle.

Finally, when she figured she couldn't hide out in there any longer without being completely obvious, she slowly made her way out of the restroom. She bent down to take a drink from the water fountain and when she straightened, she bumped into a tall, absolutely exquisite-looking man in a military uniform. Her eyes narrowed as she took in his features. There was no way to describe him but perfect—bright blue eyes, full lips, dark-blond hair, and his face was just regal with manly lines, yet he was definitely a pretty boy. Captain Levi Turner. Welcome home, jerkbait.

"Excuse me." She tried to back away, but ran into the drinking fountain.

His full lips turned up in a welcoming smile. "No, excuse me. I've been on a plane or in an airport for the past thirty-seven hours and I'm a little tipsy."

She returned the smile before she could consciously stop herself.

He didn't remember her. That stung, but they had only had that one conversation on FaceTime and she'd been so livid, her face had prob ably been distorted. Plus, she knew he would be here and in uniform, but he probably wasn't expecting her to be part of the welcoming committee.

"Nothing as miserable as being stuck in a plane or an airport," she said.

His smile disappeared. "Actually there is, it's called Afghanistan."

"Just returning home?"

"Yes. Thank heavens."

"Thank you for your service." It came out all breathy like she was an Air Force groupie or something. Yes, men in uniform were hot and she was grateful to all of them. Unfortunately, Levi Turner was one of the hottest men she'd ever seen, but she didn't like this guy, even if he was an accomplished doctor and had served their country faithfully.

He nodded, seeming uncomfortable with the praise. "Hey. I'm kind of out of practice when it comes to meeting beautiful women, but I'd love to, um ... go to dinner or something with you?"

Caylee couldn't help but let out a small laugh. His awkwardness was endearing, but when he figured out who she was he'd be ticked at himself for hitting on her, and probably ticked at her for not telling him.

At least the makeup touchup seemed to have worked, as he had just called her beautiful. "How about right now?"

"Oh." He grimaced. "I can't right now. The family's all here to welcome me home." He pointed over at the baggage claim where Cam, Sage, and Sage's parents were waiting. "We're supposed to go to—"

"In 'n Out Burger?" she supplied, hiding a smile.

"Yeah." He brushed a hand through his short locks and Caylee found herself wondering what they would feel like under her fingertips. She'd seen a picture of him with longer hair and it had about done her in. She loved long hair on men. Levi was just too good-looking to be such a punk. "It used to be my favorite," he continued, "and I haven't had a decent hamburger and fries in eighteen months, so my sister suggested we go there." He smiled at her and the full effect of that made her knees go a little gooey. "How did you guess?"

"I have a brother. We ate at that place after every lacrosse game in high school and college." She should stop this now. She was having a civil conversation with a man she'd sworn to hate, and when he found out who she was, he was going to be mad.

"It's definitely boy heaven." He flicked his thumb against his hand. "Would you give me your number?"

"Pretty brave. I know you're a military man so I *should* be able to trust you, but I might be a mass murderer for all you know." He had no way of knowing the full-extent of her lying tongue—she never trusted a man she didn't know.

He laughed. "I think I could handle a little thing like you."

"Hmm." She arched her eyebrows. Ah, and just like that the cocky man she'd expected to loathe surfaced. "If you're willing to risk your life, I'm game. Shall we meet in a public, well-lit place to keep you safe?" The type of place she met all her dates. She knew this date was never going to happen, but it was just too fun to tease him.

His grin crinkled the skin around his eyes. "You name it and I'll be there. Do you live in Salt Lake?"

"Park City actually. Home for a couple of months then I'm going back to L.A. to finish my doctorate degree."

"Impressive. What's your degree in?"

Sage appeared and wrapped her arm around Levi's waist. "You officially met Caylee."

Caylee hadn't even noticed her coming, so wrapped up in this guy's handsome mug, and actually having fun flirting with him.

"Caylee?" Levi's eyes darted from his sister to Caylee then back again. His brow squiggled. "Cam's sister?"

Caylee curtsied and grinned at him. "In the flesh."

Sage smiled encouragingly. "I'm so glad you two are getting along. Thank you. It means a lot to Cam and me that you become friends."

Levi's eyes had narrowed, but he gave Sage a squeeze and muttered, "Yeah, sure. Caylee and I are going to be *great* friends."

Sage's smile widened. "Your luggage is here. You all ready to go?"

"Sure." Levi was completely focused on Caylee's face. "We'll be right there."

She looked uncertainly between the two of them then walked back to where Cam and her parents had all the suitcases between them.

Caylee moved to dart around Levi, but he caught her arm. She glanced up, his blue eyes were sparking fire at her. "You knew who I was."

She shrugged. "Kind of hard to miss the famous and hoity-toity *Captain* Levi Turner."

He released her arm, but stayed in her personal space. Why did he have to smell like citrus and the ocean? Who smelled good after being on an airplane that long?

"There's the Caylee that I've known I would love to hate."

She gave him an imperious grin. Her thoughts exactly. "It's going to be so joyous hanging out with you at all the family parties and exchanging snide remarks."

His eyebrows arched up. "You hope you get that privilege. I have to give my approval of Cam first."

Caylee's stomach tightened. She pressed up on her tiptoes and got into his face. "Don't you dare ruin Cam and Sage's happiness because you just can't help yourself acting like a dipwad. You try it and you'll have me to deal with."

He smirked at her. "What's a model-looking pipsqueak like you going to do to me?"

"Just you wait. I've got tricks up my sleeve you've never seen before."

He chuckled and it ticked her off. "Tricks I believe, but I doubt their effectiveness."

"Don't turn your back, pretty boy."

He laughed louder still. "I won't. Oh, and forgive my massive brain lapse in asking you out. I'd rather do another tour in Afghanistan than go out with a feisty, bratty woman."

"You would only be so lucky to have a chance with someone like me." Even as she said it her insides were tumbling. She used to dream of finding a man who she could love, but that ship had sunk and she was perfectly happy with her life. Especially happy to not be dating a jerk like Levi.

"Lucky." He chuckled drily. "That's right. The man who has to endure you for a lifetime is one lucky sucker."

"Cay?" Cam's voice came from behind Levi. "Everything okay?"

Caylee gave Levi one more haughty look then scooted around him. The sight of her burly older brother helped her find her inner peace again. Levi had no power over her and she could only pray that he wouldn't jeopardize her brother's happiness.

"Yeah. Ready to go eat a slab of cow?" Caylee asked.

"Yes, ma'am." Cam grinned at her then focused on Levi. "Sage and I really hope you two will become good friends." The slightly veiled threat was there in his voice and steely gaze and Caylee loved him for it. He wouldn't put up with Levi treating her like crap, even though this loser was going to be his future brother-in-law.

Levi smiled tightly. "I'm looking forward to that, too."

Caylee rolled her eyes at him from behind Cam's back and hurried away to find Sage. Cam could deal with Levi and she would just try to stay far away from him.

Levi watched Cam's sister throughout their meal at In 'n Out Burger. She was absolutely breathtaking with her deep blue eyes, heart-shaped face, smooth, tanned skin, and crazy curls that were brown, gold, and red. Her hair fit her personality—wild and unaccommodating. He couldn't believe he hadn't recognized her and had been so taken in by her next to the drinking fountain at the airport. She must've been laughing at him on the inside. His stomach tightened and he vowed to get back at her.

He forced his eyes away from her and sank his teeth into his second double-double burger—onions, meat, special sauce—it all blended together perfectly. He'd definitely missed American food. He glanced across the table at his parents, quietly taking in the conversation. He'd missed them more than the food, but it ripped at him that his dad seemed to have shrunken over the past eighteen months with his illness.

Sage lifted her left hand to wipe some hair from her face and the large square diamond on her ring finger sent a wave of apprehension through him. Sage getting married? She grinned at her fiancé and leaned closer to him. They looked like a happy couple, but was this guy really worthy of Levi's sister? Especially with Cam's sister being a complete brat? Why should Sage have to put up with a sister-in-law like Caylee her entire life?

"So." Levi inclined his chin toward Sage's finger. "I thought I had to give approval before you got engaged."

Cam wrapped an arm around Sage and smiled. "We decided it was easier to ask forgiveness than permission."

Levi didn't laugh along with his parents and Sage.

Caylee's eyes darkened to midnight blue and narrowed at him. "What right do you have to determine someone's happiness?"

The table went silent.

"My sister's happiness is all I care about," Levi returned evenly. He stayed focused on Caylee. Always keep the enemy in your sights.

"And my brother makes her happy." She folded her arms across her chest and Levi was temporarily distracted. He'd been around women in uniform for too long. V-neck shirts were really nice-looking. He forced himself to focus back on her face.

"I'll decide that," he said.

"Levi," his mom warned softly.

Sage gave an uncomfortable laugh. "Cam does make me happy, big brother. Stop acting like some hardened military man."

Levi smiled. His little sister had always been his first priority. If she was happy he would stand down, but Sage didn't know how much Levi had changed in the past year and a half. The bodies he'd seen ripped apart and had to reconstruct had changed him. It was a horrific world out there and the only thing that had kept him going was knowing his family was safe and happy. He didn't care how thoughtful and caring the firefighter captain seemed. Levi would watch the situation carefully and if he had to take on Cam and his sister, Caylee, to protect *his* sister, he would definitely do it. His gaze flickered to the beautiful Caylee again. She glanced quickly at his parents, as if to make sure they were distracted, then stuck her tongue out at him.

Levi couldn't hold in a short laugh. He liked her fire and having enemies lurking around was what he'd become used to. This pipsqueak wouldn't be much of a challenge, but she might help him ease back in to civilian life. He smiled. Yes, taking on the sister might prove to be fun.

Read more or buy *Reluctant Rescue* here.

TWO HEARTS RESCUE BY DANIEL BANNER

Poppy Mercier stared down her enemy. "I own you," she said, eyes held steady. "Today you're going to be the one in pain."

The treadmill stared back, its beady little red and green flashing lights taunting her, daring her to bring it.

"Oh, I'll bring it," said Poppy. "I'll make you wish—"

"Everything okay?" asked a gym employee, who had been working her way up the machines wiping them down. Her name tag read, "Alta."

Poppy cleared her throat and stepped up onto the treadmill. With an embarrassed grin, she said, "Y-yeah, sorry about that. Just psyching myself up."

"I hear you," said Alta. "Sometimes you gotta let them know who's boss." She was medium-height, a few inches taller than Poppy, had gorgeous mocha skin, and a body that made it clear she showed the machines who was boss on a regular basis.

"Here's goes nothing," exhaled Poppy, then held the up arrow and the belt picked up speed. She always used the manual option for speed and incline because she hated it when the stupid machines demanded she input her weight. It was none of their business.

At 3.3 mph Poppy had to jog to keep up. Dang her short legs. At

6.0 she pulled her finger from the button and resisted the urge to use the handrails like an old woman with a walker.

This wasn't too bad. She could keep this speed for 3.1 miles. It was her first day as a member of the gym. Hopefully the monthly fee would be enough to motivate her to finally keep going with a workout plan for once. If she could just drop ten to fifteen, then keep them off …

New city—well, old city second time around—new lifestyle, new body? The spirit was willing but the flesh was, the flesh was severely lacking oxygen and Poppy's second wind was nowhere in sight. *Any second now*, she told herself. *Push through.* Even the voice in her head was out of breath.

She stared straight ahead at the pillar in front of the treadmill. She had picked this particular machine because it was the only one with an obstructed view of the enormous mirrors.

Don't check the distance yet. A little farther.

With things so slow at the shelter, Daria could hold down the fort for an hour. Once Poppy got a few days into a habit of working out, she could take the next step and drag her butt out of bed early enough to come before the shelter opened.

A line of TVs displayed various sports shows and middle of the day talk shows. Neither held any interest for Poppy, so she put her wireless headphones in and resumed her Cami Checketts suspense novel.

As she set her phone back into the cup holder on the treadmill, Poppy accidentally glimpsed the display: .09. Not even a tenth of a mile. The self-inflicted agony was going to last all day. But she couldn't take all day, she had to get back to shelter.

She also couldn't keep up this pace. If she died on this treadmill she'd leave exactly 27 animals hanging. For the sake of the animals, Poppy decreased the speed to 5.8. It still felt incredibly fast, but it was slower than a ten-minute mile.

It had to be the elevation. Yeah, that was right, the elevation.

A bright red vehicle passed in front of the gym's windows. Poppy looked up to see a fire truck and an ambulance pass slowly right along the curb. Was something wrong? Maybe she couldn't hear the alarm over her audiobook. She pulled out one earbud and looked around for flashing warning lights and saw everyone in the gym just carrying on with their workouts.

The sound of doors slamming outside had to come from the fire trucks. Maybe someone had called 9-1-1 because Poppy looked as unwell as she felt. Poppy gripped the handrail and leaned to the side. Her hair was still in its ponytail but her face was only a few shades shy of heat stroke.

The gym doors opened and a group of firemen came in. Nope, one of them was a female, so she guessed that made them firefighters? They were all dressed in gym shorts and fire department t-shirts, and the only equipment they carried was radios. It didn't appear to be an emergency.

They could have been straight out of a beer commercial. One guy was gray-haired and one was, well, for lack of a better word, fat, but as a group they were smokin'. If she hadn't seen the Park City Fire Department vehicles pull up, she would have wondered if they were here to pose for a photo shoot. Between the six of them, they had some serious muscle and fitness going on.

It was the last one through the door who really caught her eye. He wasn't a muscle head like a couple of them, but his chiseled face and prominent cheek bones gave him a rugged handsomeness. His dark hair was buzzed on the sides, but more than long enough to run a hand through on the top.

After taking a couple steps into the gym, the fireman looked directly at Poppy, as if sensing her eyes on him. Their eyes met, introduced themselves. They didn't slide off of each other and go on their way. Her eyes and his eyes said hello, sat down for a speed-date, and ended up having a lengthy conversation, backing up all the other speed daters but still not parting ways until the event coordinator was summoned to force them apart. It was much more intimate than she was comfortable with a perfect stranger, but it still took effort to pull her eyes away.

Is it hot in here? wondered Poppy. She looked down at her phone and reached for it so she could rewind the book ... and next thing she knew she was head over heels, executing a perfectly awkward and painful dismount from the treadmill. One second she was running for her life, the next she was laying on the ground, butt in the air, staring up at her knees. The treadmill was still running, grinding against her bare back and trying to rub all of the skin off.

Oh good, at least her shirt had nearly come completely off in the display of grace.

Poppy found herself chuckling through her grimace as she pushed away from the belt of the treadmill. In the face of pain that would break most POWs, she could either laugh or shout every swear word she knew at the top of her lungs. She couldn't extricate herself from the awkward position, just push off enough to prevent third-degree abrasions. Hopefully.

A few second later someone ran up, hit the emergency stop, and braced her until the torture device stopped spinning its belt.

"You didn't have to do that," grunted Poppy. "I was kind of looking forward to having my back covered in skin grafts."

"Here," said a man's voice. A hand reached through her tangle of legs and grabbed her hand. It was a man's hand for sure, solid and much larger than hers. "Lean to your left and we'll get you right-side up." Another hand rested against her knee and moving in harmony, they guided her so that she was lying on her side, finally able to breathe normally.

Poppy's ponytail had exploded and her hair now obscured every-thing. "Maybe I'll just breathe for a minute?" It was impossible to tell if the labored breathing was due to the exercise or the feat of unimagin-able poise.

"Let me just ..." Someone started adjusting her shirt, pulling it down over what Poppy's mother referred to as her "disproportionate roundness".

"Okay, then," said Poppy, shooting up to a sitting position, realizing abruptly how exposed she was. She did a quick check to make sure her sports bra hadn't somehow been splattered across the wall behind her, and breathed a little easier when her hand brushed the strap. While she pulled her shirt to a state of public decency, she flipped her head back to clear her hair out of her eyes.

It smacked the hot fireman in the face. The hot one with the eyes.

For a second he sat there, eyes closed, mouth open. Stunned. Then he lifted an arm to wipe the residue of her sweaty hair off of his face.

Nice one, Poppy. You've reached an entirely new level of smooth.

"Well, Cap," said the huge-fat fireman to the huge-muscular fireman. "Looks like Booter gets to fill out his first exposure report when we get back."

"Funny, JFK," said the man she had drenched with her mop. Looking back at her, he said, "I'm Slade. I'm an EMT. Did you hurt yourself?" He was crouching next to her as the rest of his crew gathered behind him.

Poppy somehow looked away from his dark blue eyes. "Hurt myself? What do you mean? Isn't that how everyone dismounts from these instruments of torture?" The abrasion on her back stung, especially with her sweaty shirt laying across it, but there was nothing the fireman could do about the pain.

"It's one way to do it," said Slade. "I won't judge. Here, lean back against the wall." He had a small grin on his face and Poppy realized she was smiling through the blush on her own face.

With his help, Poppy was able to relax against the wall, keeping the raw skin on her lower back arched away. "I'll just finish my workout down here. Since you didn't let me complete the dermabrasion session."

"She seems fine," said the one Slade had called JFK.

When Slade looked over his shoulder at him, Poppy couldn't prevent her eyes from quickly dipping to Slade's arms. The t-shirt wasn't skin tight, but it was tight enough to tell that the gym wasn't the torture chamber to him that it was to her. Was he flexing? He had to be flexing.

As he turned back to Poppy she brought her eyes up to his face.

"Would you like me to check you out?" he asked.

Check you out? Had he noticed the way she had ogled him when she thought she could get away with it? As in, *My eyes are up here, ma'am.* The lady firefighter and the muscle head looked at each other, focusing.

Oh no. They saw me checking him out.

The muscle head bent his ear toward the radio, which was blaring something that Poppy couldn't follow. "That's us," he said.

The female nodded. "Behind the Rite-Aid."

They all started jogging toward the exit. Except for Slade, who was still looking at her. "Are you sure you're okay? We can send another unit to that call if you need us."

From the doors of the gym, JFK yelled back, "Get on the rig, Boot!"

Slade didn't budge, still waiting on her expectantly.

"Go," said Poppy, smiling and hoping it looked thankful and not like a creepy Joker smile. "I'm fine."

"Okay," said Slade, rising. "Call us back if you change your mind. You know our number."

She watched him jog with the grace of a dancer to the door. Oh man did she watch him. Why, in the name of all the exercise gods, did that have to happen at that moment? Riding the treadmill wave like an epileptic cow in front of the gym-goers was bad enough. But no, that wasn't good enough for Poppy Mercier. She had to do it in front of a gaggle of good looking men. A herd of hotties. A flock of fire—

"Can I give you a hand up?" Alta was back, offering a hand.

Nice of her to wait until Poppy was done admiring Park City's Finest. No wait, Finest was for police, wasn't it? These guys were the Bravest. Though Poppy hadn't met many finer than that Slade.

"I love it when they come in," said Alta with a sly smile, helping Poppy to her feet.

"Oh, they're regulars?" Poppy tried to sound casual.

"Yeah, they come in and play wallyball about once a week."

"Oh good," said Poppy. "I think that dismount was only about an eight-point-five. Next week I think I can pull off a ten if I land face down on the treadmill instead of head down on the ground." She reached up and felt the goose egg forming on the back of her head. At least she hadn't cracked her head all the way open. But hey, Slade would be back in a week or so. That might be enough extra motivation to keep Poppy coming back here.

"It looked pretty painful," said Alta.

"Yeah, but in an agile, attractive sort of way, right?" The sting of sweat on raw skin hadn't faded much.

Alta laughed. "Yeah, you were as nimble as an elephant in ice skates."

"My mother's right." Poppy groaned. "I'll die single for sure."

Alta laughed again. "There's no way. A funny girl like you with such a gorgeous smile? How have you not been scooped up yet?"

It was no surprise to Poppy that she was single, but it also wasn't the time to recite the Litany of Lack. "That's nice of you to say." *Especially since you look like you should be on a magazine cover.*

"Are you feeling alright?" asked Alta. "Need to sit down, or need someone to check you out?"

"I think everyone in the gym already saw more of me than they wanted to." When she made it back to the shelter, Daria could bandage up the abrasion.

"Okay. I have some first aid training, and they give all of us a concussion class when we start working here, so I know a little bit about some danger signs."

"That's really nice of you, Alta. I'm actually a vet, so if I start walking in to glass walls or barking incessantly I'll have a pretty good idea what's wrong."

With a chuckle Alta nodded and started toward the front desk. "I'll be up here if you need anything."

Quiet enough so no one else could hear, Poppy said, "I need to show you that you can't throw me around." She put on her pit bull face, the dog, not the singer. Her enemy couldn't know that, like every one of the Pitties that had come through her rescue, Poppy was a softie inside.

Show no fear, feel no compassion.

Poppy hit the start button and took a deep breath as the machine taunted her with the three-beep countdown, and started sliding.

"Yeah, well your mom was probably a conveyor belt, and not like the cute little one at the all-you-can eat sushi. She's ... an industrial sized one in an Amazon warehouse or something."

Before the treadmill was up to speed, Poppy was too out of breath for any more insults.

I got this. Only three miles to go. Don't look down.

Miraculously her Bluetooth earbuds were still around her neck, so into her ears they went. Without crashing and burning, she found the play button and the narrator's voice picked up again.

For a while Poppy lost herself in a fictional world—a world about a running protagonist interestingly enough—and continued to remind herself to not look down. A watched pot never boils and a watched treadmill logs no miles. The rivulets of sweat started running again. She had brought a towel to wipe up after her run, but maybe that fireman would be back and she could just use his face again.

Don't look down.

If she wasn't so scared of crashing and burning again, she'd grab the towel and lay it over the display to hide it, but two catastrophic failures in one day might make it hard to show her face here again. No, the gym would probably refund her money and tell her she was too much of a liability to work out there.

Don't look ...

Poppy looked down at her adversary, expecting to be in the mid twos. Its beady little display numbers sneered back a measly .9 miles.

"Oh ... now you're just lying." Feeling like a failure, Poppy decreased the pace to 5.5. "But you know what? You can't beat me. Winston Churchill ... would give up ... before I will. I might die here, but you can't, make me stop, pounding you, until I get my, three point one."

Focus on breathing, Poppy told herself. *And don't look down.*

Read more or buy *Two Hearts Rescue* here.

RESCUE ME BY TAYLOR HART

Damon Freestone stared down at the five-mile trail run he'd just done. It had been fun. As fun as Damon could deal with at the moment. Truthfully, he hadn't even felt it. All he'd known when he'd gotten off his first full forty-eight-hour shift at Park City Fire Department was that he needed to do something to get his mind off everything.

Sucking in air, he pulled the water bottle off his hip and took a long drink. Honestly, it hadn't been that bad of a shift, considering it was his first one since he had come back from Boston. And he had been demoted to a truckie.

His mind flashed to his first day as captain six months ago in Boston, to the burning building. At this point, he usually clamped down on the memory and refocused his thoughts. At least, that was what he'd been taught to do by the stupid shrink he'd been forced to see for weeks on end after it had all happened. The one who told him none of it was his fault. After all, he'd followed protocol. Squeezing the bottle between his fingers, he crushed it and then tucked it back into the water holster at his hip. Forget the shrink.

His mind opened to that day—his first call as the captain at Boston Fire. He'd done everything right. They had vented the building first and then sent in the truck crew to make entry and start search and rescue.

They'd pulled out twenty bodies.

The fire was moving fast. He could hear his men clearing the rooms. He could see it in his mind as easily as if he'd been in there himself. They were good men, trained properly. His mind was clear as he barked out orders. Everything was going down perfectly.

Until he heard Trev call out. "Chief, she's hurt!"

At that point, it was like lightning struck his heart, and he instantly knew who Trev was talking about.

Jamie. The candidate. The new girl who had only shown up a week ago.

Without thinking, his feet went into motion.

"What the—!" He called, running to the truck and donning his air mask. He'd already had turnouts and SCBA on before they even arrived.

Corey was by his side as he moved toward the building. "Cap, you can't go in there. You have command. We need your eyes out here. There are still ten guys in there."

But come hell or high water, Damon was going in there. Time lost all meaning. He barged through the burning doors, sucking air from his tank and trying to see her, trying to feel her. He keyed his radio. "Trev, where is she?"

"I ... part of the wall has fallen up here, I can't get her out."

Climbing the stairs quickly, he rushed straight to where he'd sent Trevor. The smoke was awful, and he could barely see through it. The hungry flames snapped at him as he made his way to Trev who was trying to figure out how to get her free. Springing into action, he rushed to the beam that had fallen, using all his force to push it off, but it wouldn't budge.

On the radio, he heard the battalion chief. "Freestone, what are you doing? Get your butt out here."

He ignored it, struggling to find a way to free Jamie.

The battalion chief ordered everyone to abandon the building then started calling out his crew one by one, telling them to get out. Air horns blared long blasts of four tones, the symbol to evacuate. The fire had burned long enough that either this thing would flashover soon or the whole building might come down.

Even though Damon could feel the blow was coming, he couldn't leave yet. He scrambled to get another board and make a lever to push the beam.

Trev stayed by his side without asking and helped him push the lever.

"*Freestone! Clark!*" The battalion chief barked, calling the two of them.

Damon pointed at Trev. "Get out!"

Trev shook his head. "I'm staying with you, Cap."

The battalion chief's voice pierced the radio. "*Then you are both fools that are going to lose your jobs.*"

They pushed and levered the wood until Jamie's leg came loose. Damon picked her up and carried her out of the apartment, down the stairs and into the pandemonium outside.

The building had the decency to not flash until both he and Trev were out. Flames tumbled over their heads and the pressure forced Damon down to his knees. He climbed to his feet and ran toward the medics.

As he laid her body on the stretcher, ambo crews and firefighters swarmed them, helping them take off their equipment. Damon sucked in the cool Boston night air.

The battalion chief walked over with anger in his eyes and stared at him. "Freestone, you made the wrong call."

All Damon was concerned with at the moment was making sure Jamie was okay. He saw them intubating her.

"Is she breathing?" he asked Craig, the main paramedic.

When Craig didn't answer, he began investigating the equipment they were using, and then the other medic pulled out an AED and shocked her chest.

"Breathe." He commanded her, getting on his knees and feeling emotion bubble up in his throat. Emotion he never let out anywhere besides a punch to the face of his sparring partner at the gym in the morning.

His battalion chief was next to him, his hand on his shoulder, as

Damon watched the crew frantically try to get a pulse, get all the smoke out of her so she could breathe.

Shedding his turnouts, he hopped into the ambo with them. The medics worked efficiently, doing everything they could, but in the short ride to the hospital, he watched her unresponsive lips go blue. He watched her die.

When they pulled the stretcher out and ran her into the hospital, he ran with them down the hall, listening to the paramedics give their report to the doctors.

Can't find a pulse, too much smoke in her lungs, gave her albuterol, cortisone, a plethora of other drugs.

His mind couldn't decipher all of it. In truth, it was the first time he didn't feel absolutely involved in the scene, but more like a bystander watching it all unfold.

As he watched them cover her with a sheet, he knew it was his fault. She'd died because he'd sent her in too soon.

He wished it had been him instead.

Read more or buy *Rescue Me* here.

RESCUE MY HEART BY CHRISTINE KERSEY

"Well, isn't this just perfect?" Lacey Porter murmured as her car sput-ted before the engine shut down. Coasting onto the shoulder of the road, she glanced at the gas gauge where the needle had settled below the E, which was the kind of thing that happened when she got too focused on drawing.

Frowning, she shifted into Park, turned on the hazard lights, then pulled the key out of the ignition. Now she might be late for work. Not good.

The thought of turning up late when she was such a new employee stressed her out. Trying to calm herself, she leaned her head back and closed her eyes, then drew in a deep breath and slowly exhaled as she thought about what was going right in her life.

She had a job, even if being a waitress wasn't her lifelong ambition. Her bestie Amber was letting her room with her. And she was loving it in Park City. Even though moving there had been hard, she knew it had been the right decision.

She thought about the life she had left behind and a tentative smile curved her mouth. Most importantly, no one was telling her what to do and how to live her life. Her life belonged to *her*.

Then an image of Eric—her ex-boyfriend, the man to whom she

had given the last two years of her life—crashed into her mind. She could hear him saying that she needed to get her head out of the clouds, to pay attention to things and to stop wasting her time drawing.

Eyes flying open, she sat up straight. Shoving her long brown hair behind her ears, Lacey tried not to grit her teeth as she recalled that last ugly confrontation with Eric. The one where she'd told him she was done with him, done with the way he always ran her down, and done with his controlling ways.

Shaking her head to dislodge the memory, she focused on her surroundings. It was mid-day in early June, and as she sat on the shoulder of the road, cars whizzed by every thirty seconds or so. To her right, thick bunches of dark green pine trees filled her view while clusters of wildflowers in riots of color caught her eye. The scene reminded her that every year nature refreshed itself, which filled her with hope that she could make a fresh start too.

The image made her want to pull out her sketchpad and begin a fresh drawing. She reached toward the passenger seat where she had set her sketchpad, then paused. She didn't have time to draw just then. Especially with her car out of gas. She had to get that taken care of and get herself to work.

Caty, her boss at Caty's Cuisine, had been understanding the last time Lacey had been late, but she didn't want to push her luck. Not with how desperately she needed this job. Not with being such a new employee.

Sighing, she took her cell phone out of her purse, but then she simply stared at it. Amber was at work for a few more hours so she couldn't come get her, and with being so new to Park City, she didn't know who else she could call.

A moment later she heard a *tap, tap, tap* on her window. Startled, she whipped her head to the left and saw the most gorgeous man she had ever seen standing there. Perfectly shaped lips, strong jaw, and clear green eyes that reminded her of new shoots of grass. Not to mention the way his t-shirt emphasized his fit body and muscular biceps.

He motioned for her to roll her window down, and she lowered it a few inches.

"Do you need help?" he asked as he bent toward her window.

Feeling slightly stupid, she said, "I, uh, I ran out of gas."

He smiled, displaying perfectly straight white teeth, and she was momentarily dazzled by his beauty. "I can give you a lift to a gas station," he said. "If that would help."

Yeah. It definitely would. But she didn't know him.

Staring at him a moment, she debated about what to do as she twisted her favorite ring—her late grandmother's wedding ring—on her finger. She didn't know who else to call and she needed to get this taken care of and get to work. She didn't have a lot of options. Or a lot of money.

Tossing him a quick smile, she said, "Yeah. That would be great." Then she opened her door and got out of her car.

The man took a step back, giving her room, then he gestured to the area in front of her car where they would be out of traffic. Lacey walked to where he pointed.

The man followed her and stopped a few feet away from her. "I have a gas can. I'll run you up to the gas station and back."

Trying not to get distracted by his amazing eyes and general hotness, Lacey said, "Are you sure that's not too much trouble?" Then she told herself not to discourage him. What would she do if he walked away? Who would she call then?

"No. It's no trouble. I'm glad to help." He paused a beat. "I'm Jake, by the way."

Lacey studied his face. "I'm Lacey."

Was this really a good idea? Getting a ride from a stranger? Not sure at all, she didn't know what else to do.

The caution in Lacey's eyes was unmistakable, but that didn't bother Jake. In fact, he fully approved when a woman was skeptical about a man. He had two younger sisters and he hoped they were just as careful about the men in their lives. He also hoped they wouldn't ever take a ride from a stranger.

The irony wasn't lost on him and one side of his mouth tugged upward. Then it occurred to him that Lacey had no idea he was a good guy. That maybe she didn't want to go anywhere with him but felt that she didn't have any other options. "Or I could get the gas for you," he said. "And bring it back?"

Relief lit her eyes and Jake knew that was the right suggestion.

"I don't want to inconvenience you," she said as she used one hand to push her hair behind her ear—hair that Jake had an inexplicable desire to run his fingers through.

"I don't mind," he said. And he didn't. He was between shifts at the firehouse, and though he was on his way to buy materials for his home remodeling project, his helpful streak made this opportunity irresistible. Especially when such a beautiful woman was involved. And though he was fine with running the errand for her, he would have preferred that she go with him so he could talk to her.

A smile of obvious relief turned up the corners of her mouth, which emphasized the soft curves of her face and backlit her blue eyes —eyes which had a depth to them that fascinated him.

Yeah, he would definitely like to get to know her.

"I really appreciate it," she said. "I'll just..." She gestured toward her car. "I'll just wait in my car." Then she walked past him, and after throwing a smile in his direction, she climbed into her car and closed the door.

He figured that was his cue to leave.

Feeling dismissed, but with no reason to stick around, Jake nodded, then as he walked past her slightly open window, he said, "Back in a bit."

Moments later he was in his truck and pulling onto the road.

All the way to the gas station he thought about Lacey—beautiful, petite, quiet. Maybe he should ask her out. Why not? He wasn't dating anyone just then. Not now that Robyn was gone.

Pushing aside thoughts of the last woman he'd dated, he pictured Lacey, and again the depths he had seen in her eyes haunted him.

Just a simple date, a chance to get to know her. He wasn't looking for a romantic entanglement. Not with his crazy schedule—two days on at the station, then four days off. And not with all of the other things he had going on—remodeling his house and working part-time as a realtor between shifts. Not to mention helping Boston train for his boxing match.

It would just be for fun. Why not?

His smile grew.

He would do just that. And he was confident she would agree.

Read more or buy *Rescue My Heart* here.

ALSO BY CAMI CHECKETTS

Rescued by Love: Park City Firefighter Romance

Reluctant Rescue: Park City Firefighter Romance

The Resilient One: Billionaire Bride Pact Romance

The Feisty One: Billionaire Bride Pact Romance

The Independent One: Billionaire Bride Pact Romance

The Protective One: Billionaire Bride Pact Romance

The Faithful One: Billionaire Bride Pact Romance

The Daring One: Billionaire Bride Pact Romance

Pass Interference: A Last Play Romance

How to Love a Dog's Best Friend

Oh, Come On, Be Faithful

Shadows in the Curtain: Destination Billionaire Romance

Caribbean Rescue: Destination Billionaire Romance

Cozumel Escape: Destination Billionaire Romance

Protect This

Blog This

Redeem This

The Broken Path

Dead Running

Dying to Run

Running Home

Full Court Devotion: Christmas in Snow Valley

A Touch of Love: Summer in Snow Valley

Running from the Cowboy: Spring in Snow Valley

Light in Your Eyes: Winter in Snow Valley

Christmas Makeover: Echo Ridge Romance

The Fourth of July

Poison Me

The Colony

Made in the USA
Las Vegas, NV
21 April 2024

88986252R00089